'Marry me.'

'Is this some kind of joke?' she demanded hoarsely.

He shook his head. 'Think about it, Catherine—see what sense it makes. It gives you security, for a start. And not just for you, but for the baby.'

She stared at him with clear, bright eyes. 'And what's in it for you?'

'It legitimises everything.' His eyes met hers. 'Whatever happens, Catherine, this child will have my name and one day will inherit my wealth.'

'An old-fashioned marriage of convenience, you mean?'

'Or a very modern one,' he amended quietly.

'And what's that supposed to mean?'

'It means that we can make the rules up as we go along.'

Sharon Kendrick started story-telling at the age of eleven and has never really stopped. She likes to write fast-paced, feel-good romances with heroes who are so sexy they'll make your toes curl!

Born in west London, she now lives in the beautiful city of Winchester—where she can see the cathedral from her window (but only if she stands on tiptoe). She is married to a medical professor—which may explain why her family gets more colds than anyone else on the street—and they have two children, Celia and Patrick. Her passions include music, books, cooking and eating—and drifting off into wonderful daydreams while she works out new plots!

Recent titles by the same author:

MISTRESS OF LA RIOJA
PROMISED TO THE SHEIKH
  (*Society Weddings* 2-in-1 with Kate Walker)
THE MISTRESS'S CHILD

FINN'S PREGNANT BRIDE

BY
SHARON KENDRICK

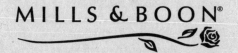

MILLS & BOON®

The character of Aunt Finola
was based on two remarkable Irishwomen—the intrepid Peggy Crone,
and my aunt, the gypsy-hearted Josephine MacCormack.

Also thanks must go to Willie Burke
for his help on the beautiful city of Dublin
and to my darling (G.V.) Schubert for his continuing inspiration!

*First published in Great Britain 2002
Harlequin Mills & Boon Limited,
Eton House, 18-24 Paradise Road, Richmond, Surrey TW9 1SR*

© Sharon Kendrick 2002

ISBN 0 263 82987 1

*Set in Times Roman 10½ on 12 pt.
01-1202-43888*

*Printed and bound in Spain
by Litografia Rosés, S.A., Barcelona*

CHAPTER ONE

AT FIRST, Catherine didn't notice the shadowy figure sitting there. She was too busy smiling at the waiter with her practised I-am-having-a-wonderful-holiday smile, instead of letting her face fall into the crestfallen lines which might have given away the fact that her boyfriend had fallen in love with another woman.

The sultry night air warmed her skin like thick Greek honey.

'*Kalispera*, Nico.'

'*Kalispera*, Dhespinis Walker,' said the waiter, his face lighting up when he saw her. 'Good day?'

'Mmm!' she enthused. 'I took the boat trip out to all the different coves, as you recommended!'

'My brother—he look after you?' questioned Nico anxiously.

'Oh, yes—he looked after me very well.' In fact, Nico's brother had tried to take more than a professional interest in ensuring that she enjoyed the magnificent sights, and Catherine had spent most of the boat-trip sitting as far away from the tiller as possible!

'My usual table, is it?' she enquired with a smile, because Nico had gone out of his way to give her the best table every evening—the faraway one, which looked out to sea.

But Nico was frowning. 'Tonight it is difficult, *dhespinis*. The table is already taken. For tonight the man from Irlandia is here.'

Some odd quality changed the tone of his voice as

5

he spoke. Catherine heard reverence. Respect. And something else which sounded awfully like a grudging kind of envy. She looked at him with a lack of comprehension. The man from *where*? 'Irlandia?' she repeated.

'Ire-land,' he translated carefully, after a moment's thought. 'He arrive this afternoon and he take your table for dinner.'

It was ridiculous to feel so disappointed, but that was exactly the way she *did* feel. Funny how quickly you established little routines on holiday. Night after night Catherine had sat at the very end of the narrow wooden deck which made up the floor of the restaurant, so close to the sea that you felt as if you were almost floating over it.

You could look down over the railing and watch the slick black waters below as they licked against the supporting struts. And the moon would spill its shimmering silver light all across the surface—its beauty so intense that for a while Catherine was able to forget all about England, forget Peter and the always busy job which awaited her.

'Can he do that?' she pleaded. 'Tomorrow is my last day.'

Nico shrugged. 'He can do anything. He is good friend of Kirios Kollitsis.'

Kirios Kollitsis. The island's very own septuagenarian tycoon—who owned not only the three hotels, but half the shops in the village, too.

Catherine strained her eyes to see a dark figure sitting in *her* chair. They said that you could judge a woman by her face and a man by his body, and, though she couldn't see much in this light, it was easy enough to tell from the taut and muscular definition of a powerful frame that this man was considerably younger than Kirios Kollitsis. By about four decades, she judged.

'I can give you next table,' said Nico placatingly. 'Is still lovely view.'

She smiled, telling herself it wasn't his fault. Silly to cling onto a routine—even a temporary one—just because her world had shattered into one she no longer recognised. Just because Peter had gone and found the 'love of his life' almost overnight, leaving Catherine wondering wryly what that said about *their* relationship of almost three years standing. 'That would be lovely. Thanks, Nico.'

Finn Delaney had been slowly sipping from a glass of ouzo and gazing out at the sunset, feeling some of the coiled tension begin to seep from his body. He had just pulled off the biggest deal in a life composed of making big deals. It had been fraught and tight and nail-biting, but—as usual—he had achieved what he had set out to do.

But for the first time in his life the success seemed empty. Another million in the bank, true—but even that seemed curiously hollow.

The ink had barely dried on the contract before he had driven on impulse to the airport and taken the first flight out to the beautiful empty Greek island he knew so well. His secretary had raised her eyebrows when he'd told her.

'But what about your diary, Finn?' she had objected. 'It's packed.'

He had shrugged his broad shoulders and felt a sudden, dizzying sense of liberation. 'Cancel it.'

'Cancel it?' she'd repeated faintly. 'Okay. You're the boss.'

Yes, he was the boss, and there was a price to be paid for that position. With power went isolation. Few spoke to Finn Delaney without an agenda these days. But, in truth, he liked the isolation—and the ability to control his own destiny which went with that. It was only when you started letting people close to you that control slipped away.

He picked up his glass of ouzo and studied the cloudy liquid with a certain sense of amusement, feeling worlds and years away from his usual self. But then, this island had always had that effect on him. It had first known him when he had nothing and had accepted him with open arms. Here he was simply 'Finn', or Kirios Delaney.

Yet for a man known in his native Dublin as The Razor—for his sharp-cutting edge in the world of business—he would have been almost unrecognisable to his many friends and rivals tonight.

The fluid suits he normally sported had been replaced by a pair of faded jeans and a thin white shirt he had bought in one of the local shops. The top three buttons were left carelessly undone, veeing down towards the honed, tanned muscle of his chest. His thick, dark hair—as usual—was in need of a cut and his long legs were stretched out lazily beneath the table.

Tonight he felt like one of the fishermen who had dragged their silver shoals up onto the beach earlier.

It was a perfect night, with a perfect moon, and he sighed as he recognised that success sometimes made you lose sight of such simple pleasures.

'This way, Dhespinis Walker,' Finn heard the waiter saying.

The sound of footsteps clip-clopping against the

wooden planks made him look round almost absently, and his eyes narrowed, his heart missing a sudden and unexpected beat as a woman walked into the restaurant. He put the glass of ouzo down, and stared.

For she was beautiful. Mother of all the Saints! She was more than beautiful. Yet beautiful women abounded in his world, so what was different about this one?

Her long black hair tumbled in ebony waves over her shoulders and made her look like some kind of irresistible witch, with a face as delicate as the filmy dress which hinted at ripe, firm flesh beneath.

Yes, very beautiful indeed. His eyes glinted in assessment. And irritated, too. Her mouth was set and, very deliberately, she looked right through him as though he wasn't there. Finn experienced a moment of wry amusement. Not something which happened to him every day of the week. He spent his life fighting off women who rose to the challenge of ensnaring one of Ireland's most eligible bachelors!

He felt the stir of interest as she took her seat at the table next to his, mere inches away, and as the waiter fussed around with her napkin Finn was able to study her profile. It was a particularly attractive profile. Small, cute nose, and lips which looked like folded rose petals. Her skin was softly sheening and lightly golden, presumably from the hot Greek sun, and her limbs were long and supple.

The pulse at his temple was hammering out a primitive beat, and he felt the heated thickening of his blood. Was it the moon and the warm, lazy night air which made him look at a total stranger and wish he was taking her back to his room with him to lose himself in the sweet pleasures of the senses? Had the magic of the island made him regress to those instant clamouring desires of his late teens?

Catherine could feel the man's eyes scanning her with leisurely appraisal, and it felt positively *intrusive* in view of the fact that he was inhabiting *her* space. She studied the menu unseeingly, knowing exactly what she was planning to have.

Finn gave a half-smile, intrigued by the forbidding set of her body and the negative vibes she was sending out. It was enough of a novelty to whet his appetite.

'*Kalispera*,' he murmured.

Catherine continued to study her menu. Oh, yes, he was Irish, all right. The soft, deep and sensual lilt which was almost musical could have come from nowhere else. His voice sounded like shavings of gravel which had been steeped in honey—a voice Catherine imagined would have women in their thousands drooling.

Well, not this one.

'Good evening,' he translated.

Catherine lifted her head and turned to look at him, and wished she hadn't—because she wasn't prepared for the most remarkable pair of eyes which were trained in her direction. Even in this light it was easy to see that they were a deep, dark blue—as wine-dark as the sea she had idly floated in earlier that day. And fringed by thick, dark lashes which could not disguise the unmistakable glint in their depths.

He had a typically Irish face—rugged and craggedly handsome—with a luscious mouth whose corners were lifted in half-amused question as he waited for her to reply.

'Are you speaking to me?' she asked coolly.

He hadn't had a put-down like that in years! Finn made a show of looking around at all the empty places in the tiny restaurant. 'Well, I'm not in the habit of talking to myself.'

'And I'm not in the habit of striking up conversations with complete strangers,' she said blandly.

'Finn Delaney.' He smiled.

She raised her brows. 'Excuse me?'

'The name's Finn Delaney.' He gave her a slow smile, unable to remember the last time he had been subjected to such an intense deep-freeze. He noticed that the smile refused to work its usual magic.

She didn't move. Nor speak. If this was a chat-up line, then she simply wasn't interested.

'Of course, I don't know yours,' he persisted.

'That's because I haven't given it to you,' she answered helpfully.

'And are you going to?'

'That depends.'

He raised dark brows. 'On?'

'On whether you'd mind moving.'

'Moving where?'

'Swapping tables.'

'Swapping tables?'

Catherine's journalist training instinctively reared its head. 'Do you always make a habit of repeating everything and turning it into a question?'

'And do you always behave so ferociously towards members of the opposite sex?'

She nearly said that she was right off the opposite sex at the moment, but decided against it. She did not want to come over as bitter—because bitter was the last thing she wanted to be. She was just getting used to the fact that her relationship had exceeded its sell-by date, that was all.

She met the mockery lurking deep in the blue eyes. 'If you *really* saw me ferocious, you'd know all about it!'

'Well, now, wouldn't that be an arresting sight to see?' he murmured. He narrowed his eyes in question. 'You aren't exactly brimming over with *bonhomie*.'

'No. That's because you're sitting at my table.' She shrugged as she saw his nonplussed expression and she couldn't really blame him. 'I know it sounds stupid, but I've been there every night and kind of got attached to it.'

'Not stupid at all,' he mused, and his voice softened into a musical caress. 'A view like this doesn't come along very often in a lifetime—not even where I come from.'

She saw a star shoot a silver trail as it blazed across the night sky. 'I know,' she sighed, her voice filled with a sudden melancholy.

'You could always come and join me,' he said. 'And that way we can both enjoy it.' He saw her indecision and it amused him. 'Why not?'

Why not, indeed? Twelve days of dining on her own had left a normally garrulous woman screaming for a little company. And sitting on her own made her all the more conscious of the thoughts spinning round in her head—of whether she could have done more to save her relationship with Peter. Even knowing that time and distance had driven impenetrable wedges between them did not stop her from having regrets.

'I won't bite,' he added softly, seeing the sudden

sadness cloud her eyes and wondering what had caused it.

Catherine stared at him. He looked as though he very easily *could* bite, despite the outwardly relaxed appearance. His apparent ease did not hide the highly honed sexuality which even in her frozen emotional state she could recognise. But that was her job; she was trained to suss people out.

'Because I don't know you,' she pointed out.

'Isn't that the whole point of joining me?'

'I thought that it was to look at the view?'

'Yes. You're right. It was.' But his eyes were fixed on her face, and Catherine felt a moment halfway between pleasure and foreboding, though she couldn't for the life of her have worked out why.

Maybe it was because he had such a dangerous look about him, with his dark hair and his blue eyes and his mocking, lazy smile. He looked a bit like one of the fishermen who hauled up the nets on the beach every morning in those faded jeans and a white cotton shirt which was open at the neck. A man she would never see again. Why not indeed? 'Okay,' she agreed. 'Thanks.'

He waited until she had moved and settled in to the seat next to his, aware of a drift of scent which was a cross between roses and honey, unprepared for the way that it unsettled his senses, tiptoeing fingers of awareness over his skin. 'You still haven't told me your name.'

'It's Catherine. Catherine Walker.' She waited, supposing there was the faintest chance that Finn Delaney was an avid reader of *Pizazz!* magazine, and had happened to read her byline, but his dark face made no sign of recognition. Her lips twitched with amusement. Had she really thought that a man as masculine as this one would flick through a light-weight glossy mag?

'Good to meet you, Catherine.' He looked out to where the water was every shade of gold and pink and rose imaginable, reflected from the sky above, and then back to her, a careless question in his eyes. 'Exquisite, isn't it?' he murmured.

'Perfect.' Catherine, strangely disconcerted by that deep blue gaze, sipped her wine. 'It's not your first visit, I gather?'

Finn turned back and the blue eyes glittered in careless question. 'You've been checking up on me, have you?'

It was an arrogant thing to say, but in view of her occupation an extremely accurate one—except that in this case she had not been checking up on him. 'Why on earth should I want to? The waiter mentioned that you were a friend of Kirios Kollitsis, that's all.'

He relaxed again, his mind drifting back to a long-ago summer. 'That's right. His son and I met when we were travelling around Europe—we ended the trip here, and I guess I kind of fell in love with the place.'

'And—let me guess—you've come back here every year since?'

He smiled. 'One way or another, yes, I have. How about you?'

'First time,' said Catherine, and sipped her wine again, in case her voice wobbled. No need to tell him that it was supposed to have been a romantic holiday to make up for all the time that she and Peter had spent apart. Or that now they would be apart on a permanent basis.

'And you'll come again?'

'I doubt it.'

Her heard the finality in her voice. 'You don't like it enough to repeat the experience?'

She shook her head, knowing that Pondiki would always represent a time in her life she would prefer to forget. 'I just never like to repeat an experience. Why should I, when the world is full of endless possibilities?'

She sounded, he thought, as though she were trying to convince herself of that. But by then Nico had appeared. 'Do you know what you're going to have?' Finn asked.

'Fish and salad,' she answered automatically. 'It's the best thing on the menu.'

'You *are* a creature of habit, aren't you?' he teased. 'The same table and the same meal every night. Are you a glutton for stability?'

How unwittingly perceptive he was! 'People always create routines when they're on holiday.'

'Because there's something comforting in routines?' he hazarded.

His dark blue eyes seemed to look deep within her, and she didn't want him probing any more. That was *her* forte. 'Something like that,' she answered slowly.

She ordered in Greek, and Nico smiled as he wrote it down. And then Finn began to speak to him with what sounded to Catherine like complete fluency.

'You speak Greek!' she observed, once the waiter had gone.

'Well, so do you!'

'Only the basics. Restaurants and shops, that kind of thing.'

'Mine isn't much beyond that.'

'How very modest of you!'

'Not modest at all. Just truthful. I certainly don't speak it well enough to be able to discuss philosophy—but since what I know about philosophy could be written on the back of a postage stamp I'm probably wise not to try.' He gazed at her spectacular green eyes and the way the wine sheened on her lips. 'So tell me about yourself, Catherine Walker.'

'Oh, I'm twenty-six. I live in London. If I didn't then I'd own a dog, but I think it's cruel to keep animals in cities. I like going to films, walking in the park, drinking cocktails on hot summer evenings— the usual thing.'

As a brief and almost brittle biography it told him very little, and Finn was more than intrigued. Ask a woman to tell you about herself and you usually had to call time on them! And less, in some cases, was definitely more. His interest captured, he raised his eyebrows. 'And what do you do in London?'

She'd had years of fudging this one. People always tended to ask the same predictable question when they found out what she did: 'Have you ever met anyone famous?' And, although Finn Delaney didn't look a predictable kind of man, work was the last thing she wanted to think about right now. 'Public relations,' she said, which was *kind* of true. 'And how about you?'

'I live and work in Dublin.'

'As?'

Finn was deliberately vague. Self-made property millionaire sounded like a boast, even if it was true, and he had seen the corrupting power of wealth enough to keep it hidden away. Especially from beautiful women. 'Oh, I dabble in a bit of this and a bit of that.'

'Strictly legal?' she shot out instinctively, and he laughed.

'Oh, strictly,' he murmured, fixing her with a mock-grave look so that she laughed too. The laugh drew attention to the fact that she had the most kissable lips he had ever seen. He found himself wondering why she was here on her own.

His eyes skimmed to the bare third finger of her left hand. No sign of a ring, present or recent. He could see Nico bearing down on them, carrying their food, and he leant forward so that the scent of roses and honey invaded his nostrils.

'How long are you staying?' he questioned.

Still reeling from the pleasure of realising that she hadn't lost the ability to laugh, Catherine let her defences down—and then instantly regretted it. Because his proximity made her heart miss a beat she blinked, startled by her reaction to the warm bronzed flesh and dazzling blue eyes. Her emotions were supposed to be suspended, weren't they? She wasn't supposed to be feeling anything other than the loss of Peter. So how come desire had briefly bewitched her with its tempting promise? 'Tomorrow's my last day.'

Oddly enough, he felt disappointed. Had he hoped that she would be staying long enough for them to forge a brief holiday romance? He must be more stressed-out than he'd thought, if that were the case. 'And how are you planning to spend it? A trip round the island?'

She shook her head. 'Been there, done that. No, I'll probably just laze around on the beach.'

'I think I might join you,' said Finn slowly. 'That's if you don't have any objections?'

CHAPTER TWO

'I THINK I might join you,' he had said.

Catherine rubbed a final bit of sun-block onto her nose and knotted a sarong around the waist of her jade-green swimsuit, aware that her heart was beating as fast as a hamster's. She was meeting Finn Delaney on the beach and was now beginning to wonder whether she should have agreed so readily.

She let a rueful smile curve her lips. She was thinking and acting like an adolescent girl! She had broken up with her long-term boyfriend, yes—but that didn't mean she had to start acting like a nun! There was no crime in spending some time with an attractive, charismatic man, was there? Especially as she had barely any time left. And if Finn Delaney decided to muscle in on her she would politely give him the brush-off.

She scrunched her dark hair back into a ponytail and grabbed her sun-hat before setting off to find some coffee. The sun was already high in the sky, but the terrace was shaded with a canopy of dark, fleshy leaves and she took her seat, trying to imprint the scene on her mind, because tomorrow she would be back in the city.

'I see you with Kirios Finn last night,' observed Nico rather plaintively as he brought her a plate of figs and some strong black coffee. Every morning he tried something new to tempt her, even though she had told him that she never ate breakfast.

18

'That's right,' agreed Catherine. 'I was.'

'He like you, I think—he like beautiful women.'

Catherine shook her head firmly. 'We're just passing acquaintances who speak the same language,
that's all,' she said. 'I'm going home this afternoon—
remember?'

'You like him?' persisted Nico.

'I hardly know him!'

'Women like Finn Delaney.'

'I can imagine,' said Catherine wryly, thinking of
those compelling blue eyes, the thick, unruly hair and
the spectacular body. She might not be interested in
him as a man, but her journalistic eye could appreciate his obvious attributes.

'He brave man, too,' added Nico mournfully.

Catherine paused in the act of lifting her cup and
looked up. Brave was not a commonly used word,
unless someone had been sick, or fought in a war,
and her interest was aroused. 'How come?'

Nico pushed the figs into her line of vision. 'The
son of Kirios Kollitsis—he nearly die. And Kirios
Delaney—he save him.'

'How?'

'The two of them take scooters across the island
and Iannis, he crash. So much blood.' He paused. 'I
was young. They brought him here. The man from
Irlandia carry him in in his arms and they wait for
the doctor.' Nico narrowed his eyes in memory.
'Kirios Delaney had white shirt, but now it was red.'
And he closed his eyes. 'Red and wet.'

Oh, the power of language, thought Catherine, her
coffee forgotten. For some reason the stark words,
spoken in broken English, conjured up a far more
vivid impression of life and death than a fluent de-

scription of the accident could ever have done. She thought of the wet and bloody shirt clinging to Finn Delaney's torso and she gave a shiver.

'They say without Kirios Delaney then Iannis would be dead. His father—he never forget.'

Catherine nodded. No, she imagined that he wouldn't forget. A son's life saved was worth more than a king's ransom. But even if he hadn't acted as he had Finn Delaney was still an unforgettable man, she realised, and suddenly the casually arranged meeting on the beach didn't seem so casual at all.

She should have said no, she thought.

But her reservations didn't stop her from picking her way down the stone steps which led to the beach. When she had reached the bottom she stood motionless. And breathless.

The beach—a narrow ribbon of white bleached sand—was empty, save for Finn himself. His back was the colour of the sweetest toffee and the lean, hard body was wearing nothing but a pair of navy Lycra shorts. Catherine's mouth felt like dust and she shook herself, as if trying to recapture the melancholy of yesterday.

What the hell was the matter with her? Peter had been her life. Her *future*. She had never strayed, nor even looked at another man, and yet now she felt as though this dark, beautiful stranger had the power to cast some kind of spell over her.

He was lost in thought, looking out over the limitless horizon across the sea, but he must have heard or sensed her approach, for he turned slowly and Catherine suddenly found that she could not move. As if that piercing, blue-eyed stare had turned her to stone, like one of the statues which guarded Pondiki's tiny churches.

'Hi!' he called.

'H-hello,' she called back, stumbling uncharacteristically on the word. But didn't his voice sound even more sensual today? Or had the discovery that another man could set her senses alight made her view him in a completely different light?

Finn watched her, thinking how perfect she looked—as though she was some kind of beautiful apparition who had suddenly appeared and might just as suddenly fade away again. A faery lady. 'Come on over,' he said huskily.

Catherine found moving the most difficult thing she had ever had to do, taking each step carefully, one in front of the other, like a child learning how to walk.

Still, he watched her. No, no ghost she—far too vivid to be lacking in substance. The black hair was scraped back and barely visible beneath her hat, emphasising the delicate structure of her face, the wariness in the huge emerald eyes.

The swimsuit she wore was a shade darker than those eyes, and it clothed a body which was more magnificent than he had been expecting. The lush breasts looked deliciously cuppable, and the curve of her hips was just crying out for the lingering caress of a man's palm.

Realising that his heart was thundering like a boy's on the brink of sexual discovery, and aware that he must just be staring at her as if he'd never seen a woman before, Finn forced his mouth to relax into a smile as she grew closer.

'Hi,' he said again.

She felt strangely shy—but what woman wouldn't,

alone with such a man on a deserted beach? 'Hi.' She
managed a bright smile. She wasn't a gauche young
thing but a sophisticated and successful woman who
was slowly recovering from a broken romance. And
as soon as the opportunity arose she would tell him
that she was interested in nothing more than a pleasant and companionable last day on Pondiki.

Finn smiled, so that those big green eyes would
lose some of their wariness. 'Sleep well?'

She shook her head. 'Not really. Too hot. Even
with the air-conditioning I felt as though I was a piece
of dough which had been left in a low oven all night!'

He laughed. 'Don't you have one of those big old-
fashioned fans in your room?'

'You mean the ones which sound as though a small
plane has just landed beside the bed?'

'Yeah.' He wanted something to occupy himself,
something which would stop him from feasting his
eyes on her delicious breasts, afraid that the stirring
in his body would begin to make itself shown. 'What
would you like to do?'

The words swam vaguely into the haze of her
thoughts. In swimming trunks, he looked like a pin-
up come to life, with his bright blue eyes and dark,
untidy hair.

Broad shoulders, lean hips and long, muscled legs.
Men like Finn Delaney should be forbidden from
wearing swimming trunks! More to distract herself
than because she really cared what they did, she
shrugged and smiled. 'What's on offer?'

Finn bit back the crazy response that he'd like to
peel the swimsuit from her body and get close to her
in the most elemental way possible. Instead, he waved

a hand towards the rocks. 'I've made a camp,' he said conspiratorially.

'What kind of camp?'

'The usual kind. We've got shelter. Provisions. Come and see.'

In the distance, she could see a sun-umbrella, two loungers and a cool-box. An oasis of comfort against the barren rocks which edged the sand, with the umbrella providing the cool promise of relief from the beating sun. 'Okay.'

'Follow me,' he said, his voice sounding husky, and for a moment he felt like a man from earlier, primitive times, leading a woman off to his lair.

Catherine walked next to him, the hot sand spraying up and burning her toes through her sandals.

The sound of the sea was rhythmical and soothing, and she caught the faint scent of pine on the air, for Pondiki was crammed full of pine trees. Through the protective covering of her sun-hat she could feel the merciless penetration of the sun, and, trying to ignore the fact that all her senses felt acutely honed, she stared down instead at the sizeable amount of equipment which lay before her.

'How the hell did you get all this stuff down here?' she asked in wonder.

'I carried it.' He flexed an arm jokingly. 'Nothing more than brute strength!'

Memory assailed her. She thought of him carrying his wounded friend, his white shirt wet with the blood of life. Wet and red. She swallowed. 'It looks...it looks very inviting.'

'Sit down,' he said, and gestured to one of the loungers. 'Have you eaten breakfast?'

She sank into the cushions. She never ate breakfast,

but, most peculiarly, she had an appetite now. Or rather, other pervasive appetites were threatening to upset her equilibrium, so she decided to sublimate them by opting for food.

'Not yet.'

'Good. Me neither.'

She watched as he opened the cool-box and pulled out rough bread and chilled grapes, and local cheese wrapped in vine leaves, laying them down on a chequered cloth. With what looked like a Swiss Army knife he began tearing and cutting her off portions of this and that.

'Here. Eat.' He narrowed his eyes critically. 'You look like you could do with a little feeding up.'

She sat up and grabbed the crude sandwich and accepted a handful of grapes, preferring to look at the chilled claret-coloured fruit than meet that disturbing blue stare. 'You make me sound like a waif and stray!'

He thought she was perfect, but that now was neither the time nor the place to tell her. 'You look like you haven't eaten much lately,' he observed.

'I've eaten well on Pondiki,' she protested.

'For how long—two weeks, maybe?'

She nodded.

'But not before that, I guess,' he mused.

Well, of course she hadn't! What woman on the planet ate food when she had been dumped by a man? 'How can you tell?'

It gave him just the excuse he needed to study her face. 'Your cheeks have the slightly angular look of a woman who's been skipping meals.'

'Pre-holiday diet,' she lied.

'No need for it,' he responded quietly, his eyes glittering as he sank his teeth into the bread.

He made eating look like an art-form. In fact, he made eating look like the most sensual act she had ever seen—with his white teeth biting into the unresisting flesh of the grapes, licking their juice away with the tip of his tongue—and Catherine was horrified by the progression of her thoughts.

When she'd been with Peter she hadn't been interested in other men, and yet now she found herself wondering whether that had been because there had been no man like Finn Delaney around.

'This is very good,' she murmured.

'Mmm.' He gave her a lazy smile and relaxed back, the sun beating down like a caress on his skin. There was silence for a moment, broken only by the lapping of the waves on the sand. 'Will you be sorry to leave?' he asked, at last.

'Isn't everyone, at the end of a holiday?'

'Everyone's different.'

'I guess in a way I wish I could stay.' But that was the coward's way out—not wanting to face up to the new-found emptiness of her life back home. The sooner she got back, the sooner she could get on with the process of living. Yet this moment seemed like living. Real, simple and unfettered living, more vital than living had ever been.

Finn raised his head slightly and narrowed his eyes at her. 'Something you don't want to go back to?' he questioned perceptively. 'Or someone?'

'Neither,' she answered, because the truth was far more complex than that, and she was not the type of person to unburden herself to someone she barely knew. She had seen too much in her job of confidences made and then later regretted.

And she didn't want to think about her new role in life—as a single girl out on the town, having to reinvent herself and start all over again. With Peter away on assignments so much, she had felt comfortable staying in and slouching around in tracksuits while watching a movie and ploughing her way through a box of popcorn. She guessed that now those evenings would no longer be guilt-free and enjoyable. There would be pressure to go out with her girlfriends. And nights in would seem as though life was passing her by.

'I suppose I've just fallen in love with this island,' she said softly. Because that much was true. A place as simple and as beautiful as Pondiki made it easy to forget that any other world existed.

'Yeah.' His voice was equally soft, and he took advantage of the fact that she was busy brushing crumbs from her bare brown thighs to watch her again, then wished he hadn't. For the movement was making her breasts move in a way which was making him feel the heavy pull of longing, deep in his groin. He turned over onto his stomach. 'It's easy to do.'

Catherine removed a grape pip from her mouth and flicked it onto the white sand. 'And what about you? Will you be sorry to leave?'

He thought of the new project which was already mounting back home in Ireland, and the opposition to it. And of all the demands on his time which having his fingers in so many pies inevitably brought. When had he last taken a holiday? Sat in such solitude, in such simplicity and with such a—his heart missed another unexpected beat—such a beautiful companion? He pressed himself into the sand, ruefully observing his body's reaction to his thoughts and just hoping that she hadn't.

Her legs were slap-bang in front of his line of vision, and he let his lashes float down over his eyes, hoping that lack of visual stimulation might ease the ache in his groin. 'Yeah,' he said thickly. 'I'll be sorry.'

She heard the slurred quality of his voice and suspected that he wanted to sleep. So she said nothing further—but then silence was easy in such a perfect setting.

She feasted her eyes on the deep blue of the sea, and the paler blue of the sky above it. Remember this, she told herself. Keep it stored in your mind, to bring out on a grey wet day in England, as you would a favourite snapshot.

She flicked a glance over to where Finn lay, watching the rise and fall of his broad back as it became gradually slower and steadier. Yes, he was definitely asleep.

His dark tousled head was pillowed on hair-roughened forearms, and the image of the sleeping man was oddly and disturbingly intimate. Very disturbing. She found herself picturing his bronzed body contrasted against rumpled white sheets and the resulting flush of awareness made Catherine get abruptly to her feet. She needed to cool off!

The sea beckoned invitingly, and she pulled off her sun-hat and ran towards it, her feet sinking into the heavy wet sand by the water's edge. She splashed her way in, waiting until she was out of her depth before she began to strike out.

The sea was as warm as milk, and not in the least

bit invigorating, but the water lapped like silk over her heated skin. Catherine continued to swim quite happily in line with the shore, and was just thinking about going in when she experienced a gut-wrenchingly sharp spasm in her leg. She squealed aloud with the shock and the pain.

She tried to keep swimming, but her leg was stubbornly refusing to work. She opened her mouth to call out, but as she did salt water gushed in and she began to choke.

Don't panic, she told herself—but her body was refusing to obey her. And the more the leg stiffened, the more water poured into her mouth, and she began to flail her arms uselessly and helplessly as control slipped away...

Finn was lost in a warm world of sensation, inhabited by a green-eyed siren with a cascade of black hair, when his dream was punctured by a sound he could not recognise. His eyes snapped open to find Catherine gone.

Instinct immediately warned him of danger and he leapt to his feet, his blue eyes scanning the horizon until he saw the disturbed water and the thrash of limbs which told him that she was in the sea.

And in trouble.

He ran full-pelt into the sea, his muscular legs jumping the waves, breaking out into a powerful crawl which ate up the distance between them.

'Catherine!' he called. 'For God's sake, keep still—I'm on my way!'

She barely heard him, even though she registered the command somewhere in her subconscious. But her body was not taking orders from her tired and confused mind and she felt herself slipping deeper...

ever deeper...choking and gagging on the sour, salty taste.

'Catherine!' He reached her and grabbed hold of her, hauling her from beneath the surface and throwing her over his shoulder. He slapped the flat of his palm hard between her shoulder blades and she spat and retched water out of her mouth, sobbing with relief as she clung onto him.

'Easy now,' he soothed. 'Easy.' He ran his hands experimentally down over her body until he found the stiffened and cramped leg.

'Ouch!' she moaned.

'I'm going to swim back to shore with you. Just hold onto me very tightly.'

'You c-c-can't manage me!' she protested through chattering teeth.

'Shut up,' he said kindly, and turned her onto her back, slipping his arm around her waist.

Catherine had little memory of the journey back, or of much that followed. She remembered him sinking into the sand and lowering her gently down, and the humiliation of spewing up the last few drops of salt water. And then he was rubbing her leg briskly between his hands until the spasm ebbed away.

She must have dozed, for when she came to it was to find herself still on the sand, the fine, white grains sticking to her skin, leaning back against Finn's chest.

'You're okay?' he murmured.

She coughed, then nodded, a sob forming in her throat as she thought just how lucky she had been.

He felt her shudder. 'Don't cry. You'll live.'

She couldn't move. She felt as if her limbs had been weighted with lead. 'But I feel so...so *stupid*!' she choked.

'Well, you were a little,' he agreed gently. 'To go swimming straight after you'd eaten. Whatever made you do that, Catherine?'

She closed her eyes. She couldn't possibly tell him that the sight of his near-naked body had been doing things to her equilibrium that she had wanted to wipe clean away. She shook her head.

'Want me to carry you back to the lounger?'

'I'll w-walk.'

'Oh, no, you won't,' he demurred. 'Come here.' And he rose to his feet and picked her up as easily as if she'd been made of feathers.

Catherine was not the type of woman who would normally expect to be picked up and carried by a man—indeed, she had never been the recipient of such strong-arm tactics before. The men she knew would consider it a sexist insult to behave in such a way! So was it?

No.

And no again.

She felt so helpless, but even in her demoralised state she recognised that it was a pleasurable helplessness. And the pleasure was enhanced by the sensation of his warm skin brushing and tingling against hers where their bodies touched. Like electricity.

'Finn?' she said weakly.

He looked down at her, feeling he could drown in those big green eyes, and then the word imprinted itself on his subconscious and he flinched. Drown. Sweet Lord—the woman could have *drowned*. A pain split right through him. 'What is it?' he whispered, laying her gently down on the sun-bed.

She pushed a damp lock of hair back from her face, and even that seemed to take every last bit of strength she had. But then it wasn't just her near escape which was making her weak, it was something about the way the blue eyes had softened into a warm blaze.

'Thank you,' she whispered back, thinking how inadequate those two words were in view of what he had just done.

A smile lifted the corners of his mouth as some of the tension left him.

Some.

'Don't mention it,' he said, his Irish accent edged with irresistible velvet. But he wished that she wouldn't look at him that way. All wide-eyed and vulnerable, with the pale sand sugaring her skin, making him long to brush each grain away one by one, and her lips slightly parted, as if begging to be kissed. 'Rest for a while, and then I'll take you back up to the hotel.'

She nodded, feeling strangely bereft. She would have to pack. Organise herself. Mentally gear herself up for switching back into her role of cool, intrepid Catherine Walker—doyenne of *Pizazz!* magazine. Yet the soft, vulnerable Catherine who was gazing up into the strong, handsome face of her rescuer seemed infinitely more preferable at that moment.

Peter? prompted a voice in her head. Have you forgotten Peter so quickly and replaced him with a man you scarcely know? Bewitched by the caveman tactics of someone who just happened to have an aptitude for saving·lives?

She licked her bottom lip and tasted salt. 'You save a lot of lives, don't you, Finn Delaney?'

Finn looked at her, his eyes narrowing as her remark caught him off-guard. 'Meaning?'

She heard the element of caution which had crept

into his voice. 'I heard what you did for the son of Kirios Kollitsis.'

His face became shuttered. 'You were discussing me? With whom?'

She felt on the defensive. 'Only with Nico—the waiter. He happened to mention it.'

'Well, he had no right to mention it—it happened a long time ago. It's forgotten.'

But people didn't forget things like that. Catherine knew that *she* would never forget what he had done even if she never saw him again—and she very probably wouldn't. They were destined to be—to use that old cliché—ships that passed in the night, and, like all clichés, it was true.

He accompanied her back to the hotel, and she was glad of his supporting arm because her legs still felt wobbly. When he let her go, she missed that firm, warm contact.

'What time are you leaving?' he asked.

'The taxi's coming at three.'

He nodded. 'Go and do your packing.'

Catherine was normally a neat and organised packer, but for once she was reckless—throwing her holiday clothes haphazardly into the suitcase as if she didn't care whether she would ever wear them again. And she didn't. For there was an ache in her heart which seemed to have nothing to do with Peter and she despised herself for her fickleness.

She told herself that *of course* a man like Finn Delaney would inspire a kind of wistful devotion in the heart of any normal female. That *of course* it would be doubled or tripled in intensity after what had just happened. He had acted the part of hero, and there were too few of those outside the pages of romantic fiction, she told herself wryly. That was all.

Nevertheless, she was disappointed to find the small foyer empty, save for Nico, who bade her his own wistful farewell.

No, disappointment was too bland a word. Her heart actually lurched as she looked around, while trying not to look as though she was searching for anyone in particular. But there was no sign of the tall, broad-shouldered Irishman.

Her suitcase had been loaded into the boot of the rather ramshackle taxi, and Catherine had climbed reluctantly into the back, when she saw him. Swiftly moving through the bougainvillaea-covered arch, making a stunning vision against the riotous backdrop of purple blooms.

He reached the car with a few strides of those long legs and smiled.

'You made it?'

'Just about.'

'Got your passport? And your ticket?'

If anyone else had asked her this she would have fixed them with a wry look and informed them that she travelled solo most of the time, that she didn't need anyone checking up on her. So why did she feel so secretly pleased—protected, almost? 'Yes, I have.'

He ran his long fingers over the handle of the door. 'Safe journey, Catherine,' he said softly.

She nodded, wondering if her own words would come out as anything intelligible. 'Thanks. I will.'

'Goodbye.'

She nodded again. Why hadn't he just done the decent thing and not bothered to come down if that was all he was going to say? She tried to make light of it. 'I'll probably be stuck in the terminal until next week—that's if this taxi ever gets me there!'

He raised his dark brows as he observed the bonnet, which was attached to the car with a piece of string. 'Hmmm. The jury's out on that one!'

There was a moment's silence, where Catherine thought he was going to say something else, but he didn't. On impulse, she reached into her bag for her camera and lifted it to her eye. 'Smile,' she coaxed.

He eyed the camera as warily as he would a poisonous snake. 'I never pose for photos.'

No, she didn't imagine that he would. He was not the kind of man who would smile to order. 'Well, carry on glowering and I'll remember you like that!' she teased.

A slow smile broke out like the sun, and she caught it with a click. 'There's one for the album!'

He caught the glimpse of mischief in her green eyes and it disarmed him. He reached into the back pocket of his snug-fitting denims. He'd never had a holiday romance in his life, but...

'Here—' He leant forward and put his head through the window. She could smell soap, see the still-damp black hair and the tiny droplets of water which clung to it, making him a halo.

For one mad and crazy moment she thought that he was going to kiss her—and didn't she long for him to do just that? But instead he handed her a card, a thick cream business card.

'Look me up if ever you're in Dublin,' he said casually, smacking the door of the car as if it was a horse. The driver took this as a signal and began to rev up the noisy engine. 'It's the most beautiful city in the world.'

As the car roared away in a cloud of dust she clutched the card tightly, as if afraid that she might drop it, then risked one last glance over her shoulder. But he had gone. No lasting image of black hair and white shirt and long, long legs in faded denim.

Just an empty arch of purple blooms.

CHAPTER THREE

'CATHERINE, you look *fabulous*!'

Catherine stood in her editor's office, feeling that she didn't want to be there, but—as she'd told herself—it was her first day back at work after her holiday, so she was bound to feel like that. 'Do I?'

Miranda Fosse gave her a gimlet-eyed look. '*Do* you?' She snorted. 'Of course you do! Bronzed and stunning—if still a little on the thin side of slender!' She narrowed her eyes. 'Good holiday, was it?'

'Great.'

'Get Peter out of your system, did you?'

If Miranda had asked her this question halfway into the holiday Catherine would have bristled with indignation and disbelief. But the pain of losing Peter was significantly less than it had been. Significantly less than it should be she thought—with a slight feeling of guilt. And you wouldn't need to be an expert in human behaviour to know the reason why. Reasons came in different shapes and forms, and this one had a very human form indeed.

Catherine swallowed, wondering if she was going very slightly crazy. Finn Delaney had been on her mind ever since she had driven away from the small hotel on Pondiki, and the mind was a funny thing. How could you possibly dream so much and so vividly of a man you barely knew?

The only tangible thing she had of him was his

card, which was now well-thumbed and reclining like a guilty secret at the back of her purse.

'Got any photos?' demanded Miranda as she nodded towards the chair opposite her.

Catherine sat down and fished a wallet from her handbag. It was a magazine tradition that you brought your holiday snaps in for everyone else to look at. 'A few. Want to see?'

'Just so long as they're not all boring landscapes!' joked Miranda, and proceeded to flick through the selection which Catherine handed her. 'Hmmm. Beautiful beach. Beautiful sunset. Close-up of lemon trees. Blah, blah, blah—hang on.' Behind her huge spectacles, her eyes goggled. 'Well, looky-here! Who the hell is *this*?'

Catherine glanced across the desk, though it wasn't really necessary. No prizes for guessing that Miranda hadn't pounced on the photo of Nico grinning shyly into the lens. Or his brother flexing his biceps at the helm of the pleasure-cruiser. No, the tousled black hair and searing blue eyes of Finn Delaney were visible from here—though, if she was being honest, Catherine felt that she knew that particular picture by heart. She had almost considered buying a frame for it and putting it on her bedside table!

'Oh, that's just a man I met,' she said casually.

'*Just a man I met?*' repeated Miranda disbelievingly. 'Well, if I'd met a man like this I'd never have wanted to come home! No wonder you're over Peter!'

'I am *not* over Peter!' said Catherine defensively. 'He's just someone I met the night before I left.' Who saved my life. And made me realise that I *could* feel something for another man.

Miranda screwed her eyes up. 'He looks kind of familiar,' she mused slowly.

'I don't think so.'

'What's his name?'

'Finn Delaney.'

'Finn Delaney...Finn Delaney,' repeated Miranda, and frowned. 'Do I know the name?'

'I don't know, do you? He's Irish.'

Miranda began clicking onto the search engine of her computer. 'Finn Delaney.' A slow smile swiftly turned to an expression of glee. 'And you say you've never heard of him?'

'Of course I haven't!' said Catherine crossly. 'Why, what have you found?'

'Come here,' purred Miranda.

Catherine went round to Miranda's side of the desk, prepared and yet not prepared for the image of Finn staring out at her from the computer. It was clearly a snatched shot, and it looked like a picture of a man who did not enjoy being on the end of a camera. Come to think of it, he had been very reluctant to have *her* take his picture, hadn't he?

It was a three-quarter-length pose, and his hair was slightly shorter. Instead of the casual clothes he had been wearing in Pondiki, he was wearing some kind of beautiful grey suit. He looked frowning and preoccupied—a million miles away from the man relaxing with his ouzo at the restaurant table with the dark, lapping sea as a backdrop.

'Has he got his own website, then?' Catherine asked, unable to keep the surprise out of her voice. He hadn't looked like that sort of person.

Miranda was busy scrolling down the page.

'There's his business one. This one is the Finn Delaney Appreciation Society.'

'You're kidding!'

'Nope. Apparently, he was recently voted number three in Ireland's Most Eligible Bachelor list.'

Catherine wondered just how gorgeous numbers one and two might be! She leant closer as she scanned her eyes down the list of his many business interests. 'And he has fingers in many pies,' she observed.

'And thumbs, by the look of it. Good grief! He's the money behind some huge new shopping complex with a state-of-the-art theatre.'

'Really?' Catherine blinked. He had certainly not looked in the tycoon class. Her first thought had been fisherman, her second had been pin-up.

'Yes, really. He's thirty-five, he's single and he looks like a fallen angel.' Miranda looked up. 'Why haven't we heard of him before?'

'You know what Ireland's like.' Catherine smiled. 'A little kingdom all of its own, but with no king! It keeps itself to itself.'

But Miranda didn't appear to be listening. Instead she was continuing to read out loud. '"Finn Delaney's keen brain and driving talent have led to suggestions that he might be considering a career in politics." Wow!' Her face took on a hungry look. 'Are you seeing him again, Catherine?'

'I—I hadn't planned to.' He had told her to drop by if ever she was in Dublin—but you couldn't really get more offhand than that, could you? Besides, if he had his very own appreciation society then she was likely to have to join a very long queue indeed!

'Did he ask you out?'

Catherine shook her head. 'No. He just gave me

his card and said to call by if I happened to be passing, but—'

'But?'

'I don't think I'll bother.'

From behind her spectacles Miranda's eyes were boring into her. 'And why not?'

'Millions of reasons, but the main one being that it's not so long since I finished with Peter. Or rather,' she corrected painfully, 'Peter finished with me. It went on for three years and I need to get over it properly.' She shrugged, trying to rid her mind of the image of black hair and piercing blue eyes and that body. Trying in vain to imprint Peter's there instead. 'A sensible person doesn't leap straight from one love affair to another.'

'No one's asking you to have a love affair!' exploded Miranda. 'Whatever happened to simple friendship?'

Catherine couldn't explain without giving herself away that a woman did not look at a man like Finn Delaney and think friendship. No, appallingly, her overriding thought connected with Finn Delaney happened to be long, passionate nights together. 'I'm not flying to Dublin to start a tenuous new friendship,' she objected.

'But this man could be a future prime minister of Ireland!' objected Miranda with unaccustomed passion. 'Imagine! Catherine, you *have* to follow it up! You're an attractive woman, he gave you his card— I'm sure he'd be delighted to see you!'

Catherine narrowed her eyes suspiciously. 'It isn't like you to play matchmaker, Miranda—you once said that single people gave more to their job! Why are you so keen for me to see Finn Delaney?'

'I'm thinking about our readers—'

Everything slotted into place. 'Then don't,' warned Catherine. 'Don't even *think* about it. Even if I was— even if I *was* planning to call in on him—there's no way that I would dream of writing up a piece about it, if that's the way your devious mind is working!'

Miranda bared her teeth in a smile. 'Oh, don't take things so seriously, girl! Why don't you just go?' she coaxed. 'Give yourself a treat for a change.'

'But I've only just got back from my holiday!'

'We can do a feature on the city itself—the whole world loves Dublin at the moment—you know it does! The single girl's guide! How about if we call it an assignment? And if you want to call in on Finn Delaney while you're there—then so much the better!'

'I'm not writing anything about him,' said Catherine stubbornly, even while her heart gave a sudden leap of excitement at the thought of seeing him again.

'And nobody's asking you to—not if you don't want to,' soothed Miranda. 'Tell our readers all about the shops and the restaurants and the bands and who goes where. That's all.'

That's all, Catherine told herself as her flight touched down at Dublin airport.

That's all, she told herself as she checked into the MacCormack Hotel.

That's all, she told herself again, as she lifted the phone and then banged it straight down again.

It took three attempts for the normally confident Catherine to dial Finn Delaney's number with a shaking finger.

First of all she got the switchboard.

'I'd like to speak to Finn Delaney, please.'

'Hold the line, please,' said a pleasantly spoken girl with a lilting Dublin accent. 'I'll put you through to his assistant.'

There were several clicks on the line before a connection was made. This time the female voice did not sound quite so lilting, and was more brisk than pleasant.

'Finn Delaney's office.'

'Hello. Is he there, please? My name is Catherine Walker.'

There was a pause. 'May I ask what it is concerning, Miss Walker?'

She didn't want to come over as some desperado, but didn't the truth *sound* a little that way? 'I met Finn—Mr Delaney—on holiday recently. He told me to look him up if I happened to be in Dublin and...' Catherine swallowed, realising how flimsy her explanation sounded. 'And, well, here I am,' she finished lamely.

There was a pause which Catherine definitely decided was disapproving, though she accepted that might simply be paranoia on her part.

'I see,' said the brisk voice. 'Well, if you'd like to hold the line I'll see if Mr Delaney is available...though his diary *is* very full today.'

Which Catherine suspected was a gentle way of telling her that it was unlikely the great man would deign to speak to her. Regretting ever having shown Miranda his photo, or having foolhardily agreed to get on a plane in the first place, she pressed the receiver to her ear.

Another click.

'Catherine?'

It was the lilting voice of honey pouring over shaved gravel which she remembered so well. 'Hi, Finn—it's me—remember?'

Of course he remembered. He'd remembered her for several sweat-sheened and restless nights. A few nights too long. And that had been that. He'd moved on, hadn't expected to hear from her again. Nor, it had to be said, had he particularly wanted to. The completion of one deal made room for another, and he had the devil of a project to cope with now. Finn dealt with his life by compartmentalising it, and Catherine Walker belonged in a compartment which was little more than a mildly pleasing memory. The last thing he needed at the moment was feminine distraction.

'Of course I remember,' he said cautiously. 'This is a surprise.'

A stupid, stupid surprise, thought Catherine as she mentally kicked herself. 'Well, you did say to get in touch if I happened to be in Dublin—'

'And you're in Dublin now?'

'I am.' She waited.

Finn leaned back in his chair. 'For how long?'

'Just the weekend. I…er…I picked up a cheap flight and just flew out on a whim.'

Maybe it wasn't the wisest thing in the world, but he could do absolutely nothing about his body's re-action. And his body, it seemed, reacted very strongly to the sound of Catherine Walker's crisp English accent, coupled with the memory of her soft, curved body pressed against his chest.

'And you want a guide? Am I right?'

'Oh, I'm quite capable of discovering a city on my

own,' answered Catherine. 'Your secretary said that you were busy.'

He looked at the packed page in front of him. 'And so I am,' he breathed with both regret and relief, glad that she hadn't expected him to suddenly drop everything. 'But I'm free later. How about if we meet for dinner tonight? Or are you busy?'

For one sane and sensible moment Catherine felt like saying that, yes, she was busy. Terribly busy, thank you very much. She need not see him, nor lay herself open to his particular brand of devastating charm. In fact, she could go away and write up Miranda's article, and...

'No, I'm free for dinner,' she heard herself saying.

He resisted a small sigh. She had been aloof on Pondiki, and that had whetted an appetite jaded by the acquiescence of women in general. For a man unused to having a woman say no to him, the novelty had stirred his interest. And yet here she was—as keen and as eager as the next woman.

But he thought of her big green eyes, hair which was as black as his own, and the small sigh became a small smile.

'Where are you staying?'

'MacCormack's.'

'I'll pick you up around seven.'

Catherine waited for him to say, Does that suit you? But he didn't. In fact, there was nothing further than a short, almost terse 'Bye' and the connection was severed.

She replaced the receiver thoughtfully. He sounded different. Though of course he would. People on holiday were less stressed, more relaxed. So was the fisherman with the lazy smile and sexy eyes simply a one-day wonder?

For her sanity's sake, she hoped so.

The morning she assigned to culture, and then she ate lunch in the requisite recommended restaurant. The rest of the afternoon she spent soaking up the city—marvelling at the shops in Grafton Street, studying the sparkling waters of the Liffey, just getting a feel for Ireland's beautiful capital city—before going back to the hotel to write up her copy.

It certainly has a buzz, she thought, as she reluctantly dragged her body from a bath which was filled right up to the top with scented bubbles.

She dressed with more care than usual. She wanted to appear all things. Demure, yet sexy. Casual, yet smart. To look as though she hadn't gone to any trouble, yet as though she'd stepped out from one of the pages of her own magazine! You ask too much of yourself, Catherine, she told herself sternly.

She decided on an ankle-length dress of cream linen, stark and simple, yet deliciously cut. Understated, stylish, and not designed to appear vampish. Not in the least.

Her black hair she caught up in a topknot, to show long jade earrings dangling down her neck, and at just gone seven she went down to the foyer with a fast-beating heart.

He wasn't there.

The fast beat became a slam of disappointment, and her mind worked through a tragic little scenario.

What if he had stood her up?

Well, more fool her for her impetuosity!

Catherine walked across the marbled space and

went to gaze at the fish tank. The exotic striped fish swam in leisurely fashion around the illuminated waters, and she watched their graceful tails undulating like a breeze on a cornfield. How uncomplicated life as a fish must be, she thought.

'Catherine?'

She turned around, startled and yet not startled to hear the rich Irish brogue which broke into her thoughts, and there stood Finn Delaney—looking the same and yet not the same. Some impossibly beautiful and yet impossibly remote stranger. Which, let's face it, she reminded herself, was exactly what he was.

He was dressed similarly to the shot she had seen on the website, only the suit was darker. Navy. Which somehow emphasised the blue of his eyes. And with a silk tie, blue as well—almost an Aegean blue. The tie had been impatiently pulled away from the collar of his shirt so that it was slightly askew—and that was the only thing which detracted from the formal look he was wearing.

Even his hair had been cut. Not short—certainly not short—but the dark, wayward black locks had been tidied up.

Gone was the fisherman in the clinging, faded denim and the gauze-thin shirt. And gone too was the careless smile. Instead his luscious lips were curved into something which was mid-way between welcoming and wary.

'Well, hi,' he murmured.

Oh, hell—if ever she'd wished she could magic herself away from a situation it was now. What the hell had possessed her to come? To ring him? To arrange to meet him when clearly he was regretting ever having handed her his wretched business card in the first place?

'Hi,' she said back, trying very hard not to let the rich Irish brogue melt over her.

He gave a little shake of his shoulders as he heard the faint reprimand in her voice. 'Sorry I'm late—I was tied up. You know how frantic Friday afternoons can be before the weekend—and the traffic was a nightmare.'

He was trotting out age-old excuses like an unfaithful husband! 'I should have given you my mobile number—then you could have cancelled.' She raised her eyebrows, giving him the opt-out clause. 'You still could.'

Finn relaxed, and not just because by offering to retreat she had made herself that little bit more desirable. No, the renewed sight of her had a lot to do with it. He *had* been regretting asking her to call by, but mainly because he hadn't imagined that she would. Not this soon.

Yet seeing her again reminded her of the heart-stopping effect she seemed to have on him. With an ache he remembered her in that stretchy green swimsuit, which had clung like honey to the lush curves of her breasts and hips. He remembered the heated cool of her flesh as the droplets of sea-water had dried on contact with his own. And the dark hair which had been plastered to her face, sticking to its perfect oval, like glue.

Yet tonight, in the spacious foyer of the up-market hotel, she couldn't have looked more different. She looked cool and untouchable and—perversely—all the more touchable just for that.

Her hair was caught back in some stark and sleek

style which drew attention to the pure lines of her features. The small, straight nose. The heart-shaped bow of a mouth which provoked him with its subtle gleam. High cheekbones which cast dark, mysterious shadows over the faintly tanned skin, and of course the enormous green eyes—fathomless as the sea itself.

'What? Turn you away when you've travelled so far?' he teased her mockingly.

She raised her eyebrows. 'From London, you mean, Finn? It's not exactly at the far end of the globe.'

'Is that so?' he smiled. 'Well, thanks for the geography lesson!'

His voice was so low and so rich and so beguiling that she thought he would instantly get a career in voice-overs if he ever needed money quickly. Though, judging by the information on the website, he wasn't exactly short of cash.

Reluctantly, she found herself smiling back. 'You're welcome.'

Finn's blue eyes gleamed. 'Do I take that to mean you don't want Finn Delaney's tour of Dublin's fair city?'

No. She meant that she was beginning to regret having come, but she understood exactly what had brought her so irresistibly. Or rather, who. In a plush Dublin hotel foyer Finn Delaney's attraction was no less potent than when he had hauled her flailing from the sea. When she had clung to his nearly naked body on a sun-baked Greek beach.

She swallowed. 'I thought we were having dinner. Not playing tourist.'

'Sure,' he said slowly. 'Are you hungry?'

'Starving.' It wasn't really the truth, nor even close

to it, but she was here now, and at least dinner would provide distraction techniques. She could busy herself with her napkin and sip at her wine and hope that the buzz of the restaurant would dilute his overpowering presence. Then maybe the evening would be quickly over and she could forget all about him.

'Then let's go.'

'Finn—'

The hesitant note in her voice stilled him. 'What?'

'You must let *me* buy *you* dinner.'

His eyes narrowed. 'Why?'

She shrugged awkwardly. Surely in some small way she could repay the debt she owed him, and in doing so give herself a legitimate reason for being here? 'I owe you. Don't forget, you saved my—'

'No!'

The single word cut across her stumbled sentence and in that moment she got an inkling of what it would be like to cross this man, was glad that she wouldn't.

'*I'm* buying dinner,' he said unequivocably. '*I* invited you and it's my territory.' His eyes narrowed. 'Oh, and Catherine—it was no big deal. You had a little cramp and I pulled you out of the water, okay? Let's draw a line under it and forget it, right?'

She wondered if there was anything more attractive than a modest hero, but she heard the determination which underpinned the deep voice and nodded her head with an obedience which was unusual for her. 'Right,' she agreed.

His face relaxed into a smile and his gaze was drawn to the direction of her feet. Flat heels, he noted. 'You wore sensible shoes, I see.'

He made her feel like Little Miss Frump! 'I didn't

wear spindly stilettos in case we were walking to the restaurant!' she returned.

'Good. Good because we are walking,' he replied evenly, though the thought of her wearing sexy high heels momentarily drove his blood pressure through the ceiling. 'Come on, let's go.'

They walked out into a warm summer evening, where the streets of Dublin were filled with people strolling with presumably the same purpose in mind.

'Have you booked somewhere?' asked Catherine.

Surely it would sound arrogant to say that he didn't need to? 'Don't worry, I've got us a table.'

He took her to St Stephen's Green—stunning and grand and as beautiful as anything Catherine had ever seen. And tucked away, almost out of sight of all the splendour, was a small restaurant whose lack of menu in the darkened windows spoke volumes for its exclusivity.

But they knew Finn Delaney, all right, and greeted him like the Prodigal Son.

'It's your first time here? In Ireland, I mean, and in Dublin in particular?' he asked, when they were seated at a window table which gave them a ringside seat for people watching. And people-watching was what Catherine normally loved to do. Normally. Except now she was finding her normal interest had waned and she was much more interested in watching just one person.

Trying not to, she shook her napkin out over her lap instead. 'Yes, it is.' Did he think she had flown out especially to see him? Some kind of explanation seemed in order. She shrugged. 'You said it was the most beautiful city in the world, and I thought I'd come and see for myself.'

He gave a low laugh. 'I'm flattered that you took my word for it.' Dark eyebrows were raised, and blue eyes sizzled into hers with a mocking question. 'And is it?'

'Haven't seen enough yet,' she said promptly.

'Haven't you?' His eyes were drawn to the curve of her breasts. 'Well, we'll have to see what we can do about that.'

CHAPTER FOUR

WHICH was how Catherine came to be sitting in Finn Delaney's sports-car late the following morning, with the breeze turning her cheeks to roses and the sky like a blue vault above her head.

'Don't forget to tie your hair back,' he had murmured as he had dropped her back at her hotel and bade her goodnight.

So she'd woven a ribbon into a tight French plait and was glad she had—because the wind from the open-top car would have left her hair completely knotted. A bit like her stomach.

'Where are we going?' she asked as she slid into the passenger seat beside him.

He turned the ignition key and gave a small smile. How cool she looked. And how perfect—with the amber ribbon glowing against her black hair. He couldn't remember the last time he had seen a grown woman tie a ribbon in her hair, and the result was a devastating combination of innocence and sensuality. 'To Glendalough. Ever heard of it?'

She shook her head. The way he said the name made it sound like music.

'Okay—here's your little bit of tourist information. It's a sixteenth-century Christian settlement about an hour outside Dublin—famous for its monastery. The name Glendalough comes from its setting—an idyllic valley in between two lakes.'

Idyllic.

Well, wasn't this idyllic enough? she wondered, casting a glance at the dark profile as he looked into his driving mirror.

Dinner had been bliss—there was no other way to describe it—though she supposed that this should have come as no surprise. Finn Delaney had been amusing, provocative, contentious and teasing, in turn. And if she had been expecting him to quiz her about her life and her loves and her career, she had—for once—been widely off the mark. He seemed more interested in the general rather than the specific.

Maybe that was a lucky escape—for she doubted whether he would have been so hospitable if he had discovered that she was a journalist. People had so many preconceived ideas about meeting journalists—usually negative—which was the main reason why Catherine had fallen into the habit of never revealing that she was a member of a despised tribe! At least, not until she got to know someone better.

No, it had been more like having dinner with the brightest tutor at university. Except that no tutor she had ever met looked quite as delectable as Finn Delaney. He had argued politics and he had argued religion.

'Both taboo,' she had remarked with a smile as she'd sipped her wine, though that hadn't stopped her from arguing back.

'Says who?'

'Says just about every book on social etiquette.'

'Who cares about etiquette?' he challenged, sizzling her with a provocative blue stare.

At which point she felt consumed by a feeling of desire so strong that it made her throat constrict with fear and guilt.

Surely it must be more than Finn himself that was having this effect on her? She'd met handsome, charming and successful men before—lots of them— but she couldn't remember ever being enticed quite so effectively.

And what about Peter? taunted the suddenly confused voice in her head. *Peter.* The man you expected to spend the rest of your life with.

Was the vulnerability which followed a break-up making her more susceptible than usual? Catherine squirmed uncomfortably in her seat, but Finn didn't appear to have noticed her self-consciousness.

Thank God.

Because he was looking at some squashy chocolate cake with a gleam of unfettered delight in the blue eyes.

'Wouldn't you just think that chocolate should carry a health warning?' he sighed.

'I thought it did—certainly if you eat too much of it!' She averted her eyes from the washboard-flat stomach.

He licked a melting spoonful with an instinctive sensuality which was making Catherine's stomach turn to mush.

'So everything in moderation, then? Is that right?' he observed softly, but the blue eyes were sparking with what looked like simple mischief.

'That wasn't what I said at all,' remarked Catherine tartly—but even so she could barely get her fork through her summer pudding.

Some men made deliberate remarks which were overtly sexual and which somehow made you end up being completely turned off by them. Whereas Finn made remarks which seemed to all intents and purposes completely innocent. So how come she didn't believe a word of the moderation bit? She'd bet that in the bedroom he was the least moderate person on the planet.

And Peter seemed a very long way away. In fact, the world seemed to have telescoped down into one place—and that was this place, with this man, eating a delicious dinner which was completely wasted on her...

The road to Glendalough passed through some of the most spectacular countryside that Catherine had ever seen.

'Oh, but this is glorious,' she sighed.

He shot her a faintly reproving glance. 'You sound surprised, but you shouldn't be. The beauty of Ireland is one of the best-kept secrets in the world. Didn't you know that, Catherine?'

And so were Ireland's men, if this one was anything to go by. 'I live to learn,' she said lightly.

And how he enjoyed teaching her, he thought, desire knifing through him in a way which made him put his foot down very hard on the accelerator.

She intrigued him, and he couldn't for the life of him work out why. Surely it couldn't *just* be a passing resemblance to a woman he had known so long ago that it now seemed like another lifetime. Or her cool, unflappable manner, or the way she parried his remarks with witty little retorts of her own, the way women so rarely did. But then, she did not know him, did she? Finn's reputation went before him in the land of his birth, and he was used to women—even intelligent ones—being slightly intimidated by that.

'Are you English?' he asked suddenly, as he slowed the car to a halt in Glendalough.

She turned to look at him. 'What an extraordinary question! You know I am!'

'It's that combination of jet hair and green eyes and pale skin,' he observed slowly. 'It isn't a typically English combination, is it?'

Catherine reached for her handbag, the movement hiding her face. Any minute and he would start asking her about her parentage, and she couldn't bear that. Not that she was ashamed—she wasn't. Of course she wasn't. But the moment you told someone that you might be descended from almost anyone but that you would never know—well, their attitude towards you changed. Inevitably. They pitied you, or looked at you with some kind of amazed horror, as if you were invariably going to be damaged by the circumstances of your upbringing.

'Oh, I'm a hybrid,' she said lightly. 'They always make for the most interesting specimens.' Her eyes met his in question. 'What about you, Finn?'

'Irish, true and true,' he murmured.

The expression in his eyes was making her feel rather dizzy, and her throat felt so dry that she had to force her words out. 'So when is my guided tour going to begin?'

'Right now.' He held the door of the car open, his hand briefly brushing against her bare forearm as he helped her out, feeling the shivering tension in response to the brief contact. Instinctive, he thought, and found his mind playing out wicked and tantalising scenes, wondering if she was an instinctive lover, if she gave and received pleasure in equal measure.

Through the backdrop of mountains she saw low streams with stepping-stone rocks, and Celtic crosses which were really burial stones. She stared hard at the primitive carvings.

'You don't like graves?' he quizzed, watching her reaction.

'Who does?' But the question still lay glinting in the depths of his blue eyes and she answered truthfully, even though it sounded a little fanciful. 'I guess that looking at them makes you realise just how short life is.'

'Yes. Very short.' And if his life were to end in the next ten minutes, how would he like to spend it? He stared at the lush folds of her lips and longed to feel them tremble beneath the hard, seeking outline of his. 'Let's walk for a while,' he said abruptly.

They walked until Catherine's legs ached, and she thought what a wimp living in a city had made her. Which just went to show that the machines at the gym were no substitute for honest-to-goodness exercise! 'Can we stop for a moment?' she asked breathlessly.

'Sure.'

They sat side by side on a large black rock in companionable silence and then he took her to a simple greystone building where refectory tables were laid out and lots of students sat drinking tea and eating big, buttered slices of what looked like fruitcake. It wasn't what she had been expecting.

'Ever eaten Champ?' he enquired, as they sat down.

She shook her head. 'What is it?' she asked.

'Potato.'

'Just potato?' She threw her head back and laughed. So much for eating out with a millionaire! 'You're giving me potato?'

He gave a slow smile. 'Well, no—there's chopped

shallots added, and it's served in a mound, and you melt a great big lump of butter in the centre. Try some.'

It was pure nursery food—warm and comforting, with a golden puddle of butter seeping into the creamy mashed potato.

'It's good,' said Catherine, as she dipped her fork into it.

'Isn't it?' Their eyes met in a long, unspoken moment. 'Where would the Irish be without the humble potato?'

'Where indeed?' she echoed, thinking how uncomplicated life felt, sitting here with him. For a moment all the stresses of Catherine's London life seemed like a half-remembered dream. There was a sense of timelessness in this place which seemed to give her a sense of being of this world and yet not of it.

And Finn seemed timeless, too—his clever eyes watching her, the tension in his body hinting at things she would prefer not to think about. Their mouths were making words which passed for conversation, but seemed so at odds with the unspoken interaction which was taking place between them.

After she had drunk a cup of tea as black as tar itself he leaned across the table towards her, smelling not of fancy aftershave but of soap and the undeniable scent of virile male.

'Would you like to see the Wicklow Bay?' he asked softly.

If he'd promised to show her the end of the rainbow she would have agreed to it at that precise moment. 'Yes, please.'

They drove through countryside as green as all the songs said it was, until Finn drew to a halt next to a spectacular seascape and switched the engine off. 'Let's get out. You can't appreciate it properly from here.'

They stood in silence for a moment, watching and listening as the waves crashed down onto the beach.

'There,' he murmured. 'What do you think to that?'

She thought of the view from her bedroom window back in Clerkenwell and how this paled in comparison. 'Oh, it's stunning!'

'But not a patch on Greece?'

She shook her head. 'On the contrary—it's just as beautiful. But wilder. More elemental.' Just like him, she thought, stealing a glance at him.

He stood like an immovable figurehead as he gazed out to sea, the wind whipping his black hair into dark little tendrils. He turned to look at her and something in the uninhibited pleasure in her eyes quite took his breath away.

'So, do you have a sense of adventure, Catherine?' he murmured.

'Why do you ask?'

'I'll guess you haven't been in the sea since your holiday?'

'Well, no. There isn't a lot of it in London!'

'And you know what they say about getting straight back on a horse after it's thrown you?'

'Just what are you suggesting, Finn?'

His eyes burned into her.

'Shall we let the waves catch us between the toes as we sink into the sand?' he asked, in a lilting voice. 'Take our shoes off and walk on the edge?'

It sounded unspeakably sensual, and unbelievably echoed the way she was feeling right then. On the edge. Yes. But the edge of what she didn't know.

'And you call *that* being adventurous?' she teased, because at least that way she could disguise the sudden helplessness she was experiencing. 'What a boring life you must have led!'

And she kicked off her sandals and took them in her hand, leaving her legs bare and brown as she looked at him with a touch of defiance. 'Come on, then! What are you waiting for?'

He was waiting for the ache in his groin to subside, but he gave a wry smile as he bent to roll his jeans up, wondering how she would react if he said what was *really* on his mind. That she might like to slip that dress right off, and her bra and panties, too, and go skinny-dipping with him and let him make love to her in the icy water? God, yes! Now that really *would* be adventurous!

Then he drew himself up, appalled. He didn't have sex in public with women he barely knew!

She ran ahead of him, wanting to break the sudden tight tension, and the sea was icy enough to achieve that. 'Yeow!' she squealed, as frothy white waves sucked up between her toes and rocked her. 'I'm going back!'

'*Now* who's the unadventurous one?' He held out his hand to her. 'Here.'

Feeling suddenly shy, she took it as trustingly as a child would, safe and secure in that strong, warm grasp. But a child would not have had a skittering heart and a dry mouth and a fizzing, almost unbearable excitement churning away inside her, surely?

'Blowing the cobwebs away?' he asked, as they retraced their steps.

'Blown away,' she answered. And so was she. Completely.

Her hand was still in his, and he guessed that to the eyes of an outsider they would look like a pair of lovers, killing time beautifully before bed.

He moved fractionally closer and whispered into her ear, as if afraid that the words might be lost on the wind. His whole world seemed to hinge on his next question and what her response to it would be. 'Would you like to see where I live, Catherine?'

She jerked her head back, startled. 'What. Now?'

He had not planned to say it. He kept his home territory notoriously private, like a jungle cat protecting its lair. In fact, he had thought no further than a scenic trip to Glendalough. But something about her had got beneath his skin.

He raised his eyebrows at her questioningly. 'Why not?' He looked at the goosebumps on her bare legs and arms and suppressed a small shiver as the tension began to build and mount in his body. 'You're cold. You look like you could do with some warming up.'

Catherine supposed that the drawled suggestion could have sounded like a variation on Come up and see my etchings, but somehow the rich, Irish brogue made it sound like the most wonderful invitation she'd ever heard.

He was right—she *was* cold. And something else, too. She was slowly fizzing with a sense of expectation and excitement—her nerve-endings raw and on fire with it.

Not the way that Catherine Walker normally behaved, but—so what? Surely it was just natural and acceptable curiosity to want to see his home? At least, that was what she told herself as she heard herself replying, 'Yes, I'd like that, Finn. I'd like that very much.'

CHAPTER FIVE

'SO THIS is where you live, is it?' asked Catherine, rather stupidly stating the obvious and wondering if she sounded as nervous as she suddenly felt.

What was she doing here, alone in a strange flat with this gorgeous black-haired and blue-eyed Irishman? Setting herself up for some kind of seduction scene? Waiting for Finn to put his arms around her and kiss her? To discover whether that kiss would really be as wonderful as she'd spent far too much time imagining?

And isn't that what you really want? questioned a rogue voice inside her head. Isn't that why your heart is pumping in your chest and your cheeks are on fire, even though you're supposedly cold?

Finn smiled. 'I bought it for the view.' But he wasn't looking out of the window.

'I can see why.' She swallowed, tearing her eyes away from that piercing sapphire gaze with difficulty.

The lit-up Georgian buildings in the square outside predominated, but she could see the sparkle of the Liffey, too, reflecting the darkening sky and the first faint gleam of the moon.

'Shall I make you something warm to drink?' he questioned softly.

She smiled. 'The cold's all gone.'

The walls of his huge flat seemed to be closing in on him, and he knew that if he didn't move he might do something both of them would regret. 'Then come outside, onto the terrace—you can see for miles.' He unlocked a door which led out onto a plant-filled balcony. 'The moon is huge tonight. Big as a golden dinner-plate and fit for a king.'

She thought how Irishmen had the ability to speak romantically without it detracting one iota from their masculinity. And he hadn't lied about the moon. It dazzled down on them. 'It looks close enough to touch,' whispered Catherine.

'Yes.' And so did she.

She forced herself to look at the pinpricks of silver stars, to listen to the muted sound of the city, knowing all the while that his eyes were on her, and eventually she turned to face the silent, brooding figure.

'It's lovely,' she said lamely.

'Yes.' He narrowed his eyes as he saw her shiver. 'You're cold again?'

'Yes. No. Not really.'

'Coffee,' he said emphatically. But he could see the tremble of her lips, and the tension which had slowly been building up inside him suddenly spilt over into the realisation that he could no more walk out into his kitchen and make her some coffee than he could resist what he was about to do next. 'But it's not coffee you want, is it, Catherine?' he questioned, and pulled her gently into his arms. 'Is it?'

Her world spun out of focus and then clicked back into perfection. 'Finn!' she said breathlessly. 'Wh-what do you think you're doing?'

He laughed softly at the predictable question, noting in a last moment of sanity that there was no reproach in it. 'Just this. What you want me to do. What those big green eyes of yours have been asking me to do from the moment I met you.' And he lowered his mouth, brushing his lips against the sudden wild tremble of hers.

She swayed against him, opening her mouth to his and feeling as though she had been born for this kiss, thinking that nothing had ever felt quite like this— not even with Peter.

Is this what all the books and magazines write about? she wondered dazedly. Is this why *Pizazz!* has such a massive and growing readership?

'Oh, Finn. Finn Delaney,' she breathed against the warmth of his breath, and the kiss went on and on and on.

He lifted his mouth away by a fraction, seeing the look on her face and feeling pretty dazed himself. As though he had drunk a glass of champagne very quickly, and yet he had drunk nothing stronger than tea. 'You were born to be kissed, Catherine,' he observed unsteadily.

'Was I?' she questioned, with equally unsteady delight.

'Mmm.' He pulled a pin from her hair so that it tumbled free, black as the sky above them. 'To be made love to beneath the stars, with the light of the moon gilding your skin to pure gold.'

'I've never been made love to beneath the stars,' she admitted, without shyness.

He smiled as he took her hand, raised it to his lips, his eyes unreadable. 'It's too cold out here, but you can see them from my bedroom.'

She didn't remember making any assent, only that her hand was moved from his mouth to his hand and that he was leading her through the splendour of his Georgian flat into his bedroom.

'See,' he said softly, and pointed to the huge windows where outside the night sky dazzled.

'It's like the London Planetarium!' she said. 'You're very lucky.'

'Very,' he agreed, but both of them knew he wasn't talking about the stars. 'You're a long way away, Catherine.'

'A-am I?'

'Yes, indeed. Come here.'

She knew a moment's apprehension as she walked straight into his arms. And now she *could* see his eyes, and read the hectic glitter in their velvet blue. What in the world was she *doing*?

But by then he was sliding the zip of her dress down in one fluid movement, as if he had done such a thing many, many times before. And Catherine supposed that he had.

'I should feel shy,' she murmured.

'But you don't?'

'You've seen me with less on than this.'

But underwear was always a million times more decadent than a bikini, however brief. 'So I have,' he agreed thickly, as he surveyed her lace-clad body. 'Only this looks a whole lot better.'

He bent his head to touch his lips against the tip of one breast which strained impatiently against the flimsy lace of her brassière.

And Catherine closed her eyes, giving herself up to sensation instead of thought. A soft, sweet aching overwhelmed and startled her, and she wound her arms tightly around his neck, as if afraid that he might suddenly disappear. As if this—and him—might be all some figment of a fevered longing. 'Oh, Finn,' she sighed.

He lifted his head and looked at her questioningly. 'Should we be doing this?' Her green eyes opened very wide.

He felt like saying that this was something she should have asked herself earlier than now, that his body was growing unbearably hard.

'That's up to you, sweetheart.' His mouth immediately stopped grazing the long line of her neck, the restraint nearly killing him. 'It's make-your-mind-up time. Stop me if that's what you want.'

Was he aware that he was asking the impossible?

'Do you want to?' he murmured.

'God, no. No,' she breathed. A thousand times no. She moved her mouth to rove over the rough shadow of his chin, her hands on the broad bank of his shoulders for support, her knees threatening to buckle.

He gave a low, uneven laugh as the moonlight shafted through the window and illuminated the ebony strands of her hair. Her undisguised need only fuelled him further, and he gave in to the overwhelming desire to possess her. His hand reached round to snap open her brassière, as though they were old and familiar lovers, and she clung to him wearing nothing but a tiny little thong.

'I want to make love to you, Catherine,' he said urgently.

She didn't reply, just burrowed her hands beneath his sweater, finding the silken skin there, her fingernails tracing faint lines against it, hearing him suck in a ragged breath.

'I want to make love to you,' he repeated. 'Come to bed.' He didn't wait for an answer, just led her over to the king-sized canopied bed and pulled back the cover. 'Get in, sweetheart,' he instructed shakily. 'You're shivering.'

Shivering? She felt in a fever of need, was glad to slip beneath the duvet—glad for its protection and for the opportunity to watch him throw his clothes carelessly to the floor, until he was completely and powerfully naked. All golden skin and dark shadows and hewn, strong limbs.

'Move over,' he whispered as he climbed in beside her, encountering the soft folds of her flesh, and he moved to lie over her. 'No, on second thoughts,' he drawled as the warmth of her body met his, 'stay exactly where you are.'

'Are you asleep?'

Finn opened his eyes. No, he hadn't been asleep. He had been lying there, alternating between revelling in the sated exhaustion of his flesh and wondering what the hell he had done. 'Not any more.' He yawned.

'Did I wake you?' She wondered if that sounded defensive, and then swiftly made up her mind that she was not going to lie around analysing what had happened. He had made love to her and she had enjoyed it. More than enjoyed it. End of story in this modern age. Not well-thought-out, not necessarily wise, but it had happened, and there was no point in trying to turn the clock back and regret it.

Finn smiled, his reservations banished by the sight of her wide green eyes and the dark, dark hair which tumbled down in disarray over her lush, rose-tipped breasts. He gave a rueful glance down at his already stirring body. 'Kind of.'

Catherine swallowed as she saw the involuntary

movement beneath the thin sheet and felt an answering rush of a warmth. Oh, God! How did he make her feel the way he did? And then she looked at him, every glorious pore of him, and the answer was there, before her eyes.

To her horror she found herself asking the worst question since the beginning of time. 'So how come you've never married, Finn?'

He repressed a sigh. Silent acquiescence was what his chauvinistic heart most longed for. He reached and pulled her down against his bare chest. 'Is that a proposal?' he teased. 'Because surely it's a little early for that kind of thing?'

She felt her breasts pressing against him, but suddenly she wanted more than this. She had spent the night making love to him. She knew his body. But what did she know of the man himself? He might have made her cry out his name time and time again, but a girl had her pride.

'Are you always so evasive?' she teased.

'I am when my mind is on other things. Like now.'

'Finn!'

'Mmm?'

He was stroking her bottom now, running the flat of his hand over it with the appreciation that a horse-lover might give to a particularly prize filly. And though her mind began to form a protest it was too late, because he had slid his fingers right inside her still-sticky warmth.

Her eyes opened very wide. 'Finn!' she said again, only she could hear the helpless pleasure in her own voice.

'What?'

'Stop it.'

'You don't want me to stop it.'

'Yes, I do!'

'Then why are you moving your hips like that?' he purred suggestively as his fingers continued to stroke and play with her.

'You know damned well why!' she moaned, feeling the sweet tension building, building.

'Still want me to stop?' He stilled his hand and looked at her half-closed eyes and parted lips.

She shook her head wildly. 'No!' she whimpered, and just the renewed touch of him was enough to make her splinter into a thousand ecstatic pieces.

He thrust into her warm, still-tight flesh, the sensation nearly blowing his mind, and his last thought before the earth spun on its axis was that nothing had ever felt this good. Nothing. He felt the violent beckoning of sweet release just as he heard her give another choked moan of disbelief, and then his blood thundered and he moaned.

She rolled off his sweat-sheened body and collapsed on the bed beside him. It took a moment for her breath to return to anything approaching normality. 'Wow,' she said eventually.

'Wow, indeed,' he echoed drily. But he felt shaken. Was it simply *because* they were virtual strangers that their lovemaking had been the best of his life? He stared sightlessly at the ceiling.

And now what? Catherine dozed for a moment or two, then opened her eyes again. 'I guess I'd better think about going.' She held her breath almost imperceptibly, wondering whether he would beg her to stay. She gave a half-smile. No, not beg. Men like Finn Delaney didn't beg—didn't ever *need* to beg, she would hazard.

'Must you?' he questioned idly.

Well, there she had it in a nutshell. He wasn't exactly kicking her out of bed, but neither was he working out a busy timetable for the rest of the day.

''Fraid so,' she fibbed. 'I have a plane to catch.'

'What time?'

'Five o'clock.'

He glanced at the wristwatch he had had neither the time nor the inclination to remove last night. 'It's only ten now.'

And?

'You'll have some breakfast first?' He turned onto his side and gave a slow smile. 'I make great eggs!'

He made great love, too. But she was damned if she was going to go through his thanks-very-much-for-the-memory routine. Dispatched with eggs and a shower, and perhaps another bout of uninhibited sex if she was lucky. Catherine Walker might have behaved recklessly last night, but at least she still had her pride.

And no way was she going to hang around like an abandoned puppy, desperate for affection!

'I'll skip,' she said casually, and slid her bare legs over the mattress. 'I never eat breakfast.'

'You should,' he reprimanded.

Perhaps she should. Like perhaps she should have thought twice about allowing herself to get into a situation like this.

'Coffee will be fine. Mind if I use the shower?'

'Of course not.'

How bizarre to be asking his permission for something like that when she had allowed him the total freedom of her body during that long and blissful night.

Had she just been feeling love-starved and re-
jected? she wondered as she stood beneath the steam-
ing jets of water in his typically masculine bathroom.
And how often did he entertain women in such a
spontaneous and intimate way?

It was a one-off for *her*, sure—but maybe she was
just one of a long line of willing women who were
so easily turned on by his captivating blend of Irish
charm and drop-dead sexuality.

Catherine repressed a shudder as she dried herself.
She didn't want to know.

She came out of the bathroom looking as cool and
as aloof as a mannequin, and Finn blinked. To look
at her now you would never have believed that she
could be such a little *wildcat* in bed. He felt another
tug of desire and despaired.

Catherine picked up her bag and went over to
where he was standing by the window, watching her
with an unreadable expression. She wondered how
many hearts he had broken in his time. Scores, un-
doubtedly—but hers would not be among them. She
would extricate herself as gracefully and as graciously
as possible.

'What about coffee?' He frowned.

She shook her head. She would not cling. Last
night had just happened; she must put it down to experience. And at least, she thought wryly, at least it
had got Peter well and truly out of her system. 'I'll
get some back at my hotel.' She gave him what she
hoped was a cool, calm smile. 'Thanks for a great
evening, Finn.' She raised herself up on tiptoe to kiss
his cheek. 'A great night, I should say,' she added,
braving it out.

'The pleasure was all mine,' he murmured.

Ruthlessly, she eradicated any trace of awkwardness or vulnerability from her voice, but it wasn't easy—not when confronted by the glittering blue eyes which reminded her of things which were making her pulses race. Even now. 'Bye, then.'

Once again her coolness intrigued him, particularly in view of what had happened—she was behaving as though she had just been introduced to him at a formal drinks party! Maybe she was trying to slow the pace down, and in view of the speed with which things had happened wasn't that the best thing to do under the circumstances? So why did he want to drag her straight back to bed?

He was just about to suggest running her back to her hotel when the telephone began to ring. He gave a small click of irritation.

'Answer it,' she urged, as this evidence of a life of which she knew nothing drove reality home. She was eager now to make her escape, to put it all down to a wonderful never-to-be-repeated experience.

'Don't worry, it's on the Ansaphone—'

It was also echoing out over the flat, and after his drawled and lilting message came the sound of a female voice. 'Finn, it's Aisling—where the hell were *you* last night?'

He leaned over and clicked off the machine, but by then Catherine was by the door, her features closed and shuttered.

'Look me up if ever you're in London,' she said, and walked out without a backward glance. She wondered who Aisling was, and where he was supposed to have been last night, before telling herself that her behaviour guaranteed nothing other than a night to remember—certainly not the right to question him.

Finn stood staring after her for a long, indefinable moment as the sound of the lift outside whirred into action, taking her out of his life just as quickly as she had burst into it.

And it occurred to him that he didn't have a clue where she lived.

CHAPTER SIX

CATHERINE spent the whole evening pacing the flat, tempted to smoke a cigarette—which she hadn't done in almost three years now. She kept telling herself that it had been out of character. True. Telling herself that it had been a terrible, terrible mistake. But unfortunately the jury was still out on that one.

Because the mind could play all kinds of tricks on you, and at the moment her mind seemed very fond of sending tantalising images of black hair, a bare, bronzed body and a pair of beautiful, glittering blue eyes. Images which kicked her conscience into touch.

She didn't want to think about him! Not when there was no future in it—and there was definitely no future in it. He hadn't exactly been distraught at the thought of her leaving, had he? Demanding to know her phone number and asking when he could fly out to London to see her?

But what did she expect? The pay-off for acting on instinct rather than reason was never going to be love and respect.

She forced herself to go through her photo albums and look at pictures of her and Peter, but instead of pain ripping through her there was merely a kind of horrified acceptance that Finn had been able to transport her to realms of fantasy which Peter never had.

So what did that say about their long-standing relationship? More importantly, what did it say about *her*?

She had only just sat down at her desk on Monday when there was a telephone call from Miranda.

'Can you get up here right now, Catherine? I want to talk to you about Dublin.'

'Sure,' answered Catherine, in a voice which was made calm only by sheer effort of will. 'I've written the piece.'

'Never mind about that,' Miranda answered mysteriously. 'Just get your butt up here!'

There was a quivering air of expectancy and excitement on the editor's face.

'Did you meet him?'

'Who?'

'Who? *Who?* Finn Delaney, of course!'

'Oh, him,' answered Catherine with monumental calm, though inside her heart was crashing painfully against her ribcage. She wondered what Miranda would say if she told her that she had spent most of her time in Dublin being made love to by Finn Delaney. Not a lot, most probably. Miranda had been a journalist for long enough not to be shocked by *anything*. Her throat felt too dry for her to be able to speak, but she managed. 'Er, yes, I saw him. Why?'

'And did he seem interested in you? I mean, like, *really* interested in you?'

It wasn't just the odd way that the last question was phrased, or that it was mildly inappropriate. No, something in Miranda's tone alerted Catherine to the fact that this was not simply idle curiosity, and she felt the first whispering of foreboding. She played for time. 'Interested in what way, exactly?'

Miranda snorted. 'Don't be so dense, Catherine—it doesn't suit you! Sexually. Romantically. Whatever you like to call it.'

'No comment.' But Catherine gave it away with the deep blush which darkened her cheeks.

Miranda looked even more excited. Everyone in the business knew what 'no comment' meant and immediately Catherine could have kicked herself for saying it. It implied guilt, and guilt was pretty close to what she was feeling.

'So he was?' observed Miranda.

'No!'

'I'd recognise that look on a woman's face anywhere—'

'What look?' asked Catherine, alarmed.

'That cat-got-the-cream look. The kind of look which speaks volumes about just how you spent your weekend!'

'Just leave it, Miranda, won't you?' Suddenly Catherine was feeling flustered, out of her depth. Her boss was the last person to make a value judgement about her behaviour, but what about the way she was judging *herself*? 'I don't want to talk about it!'

'Well, let me show you something,' said Miranda slowly, and picked up a clutch of photos which were lying on her desk, 'which might just change your mind.'

'If it's photos of Finn, you've already shown me—remember? I know he's loaded, and I know he's powerful and the next-best thing to sliced bread, but if you're looking for a kiss-and-tell story then you're wasting your time, Miranda.'

'No—look,' said Miranda with unusual brevity, and handed her one of the photos.

Catherine stared at it, and her blood ran cold as time seemed to suspend itself.

For it was like looking into a mirror. Seeing herself,

only not quite seeing herself. The same and yet remarkably different. She blinked. The woman in the photo had jet-black hair and huge green eyes, and a certain resemblance around the mouth, but there the similarities ended.

It was like comparing a piece of crude mineral deposit to the finished, highly polished diamond it would one day become.

Because the woman in the photo had all the pampered glamour of someone who spent absolute riches on herself. Someone who indulged, and indulged, and indulged.

'Who is this?' breathed Catherine.

'Deirdra O'Shea,' said Miranda instantly. 'Heard of her?'

'N-no.'

'Bit before your time, I guess—though I'd only vaguely heard of her myself. She's Irish—well, the name speaks for itself, doesn't it?—starred in a couple of forgettable films about ten years ago and has been living in Hollywood trying to make it big ever since but never quite managing it. She's your spitting image, isn't she?'

Something close to fear was making breathing suddenly very difficult. 'Why are you bothering to show me this?'

Miranda shrugged, and thrust another photo into Catherine's frozen fingers. 'Just that she was Finn Delaney's sweetheart.'

It was a curiously old-fashioned word to use, especially about a man like Finn, and it hurt Catherine more than it had any right to. 'What do you mean, his *sweetheart*?'

'He was smitten, apparently—completely and utterly smitten. They met before either of them had really made it—and you know what that kind of love is like. Fierce and elemental. Love without the trappings.' Miranda sighed, sounding for a moment almost wistful. 'The real thing.'

'I still don't understand what this has got to do with me!' said Catherine crossly, but she was beginning to get a very good idea.

'He's a notoriously private man, right?'

Catherine shrugged. 'Apparently.'

'Yet he meets you on a Greek island and tells you to look him up.'

'Lots of people do things like that on holiday.'

'And you fly out there and have some kind of red-hot weekend with him—'

'I didn't say that!'

'You didn't have to, Catherine—like I said, I can read it all over your face.' Miranda paused. 'Are you seeing him again?'

Now she felt worse than reckless—she felt stupid, too. 'I—hadn't—planned to.'

'He didn't ask you?'

No, he hadn't asked her. The truth slammed home like a blunt fist and defensiveness seemed her only rational form of protection. 'Miranda—what the hell is this all about? Some kind of Spanish Inquisition?'

'All I'm saying is that if he used you as some kind of substitute for the woman who broke his heart—'

Catherine opened her mouth to say that it wasn't like that. But what *had* it been like, then? He hadn't struck her as the kind of man who would normally make mad, passionate love to a complete stranger. A notoriously private man...

So what could have been his motivation?

She, at least, could blame her reeling emotions on having been dropped by Peter. But—dear God—had Finn Delaney spent the whole time imagining that she was *someone else*?

Her ego, already severely punctured, underwent a complete deflation.

When he'd told her she was beautiful, and how it was a crime against society for a body like hers to be seen wearing any clothes at all, had he been thinking about Deirdra? When he'd driven deep inside her, had he been pretending that it was another woman's soft flesh he was penetrating?

Inwardly she crumpled as she realised just what she had done. But most of all what *he* had done. He had used his Irish charm in the most manipulative and calculating way imaginable. He had guided her into his bed with all the ease of a consummate seducer, had made love to her and then let her walk out of his flat without a care in the world.

He hadn't even asked for her phone number, she remembered bitterly.

She came out of her painful little reverie to find Miranda's eyes fixed on her thoughtfully—with something approaching kindness in them. And Catherine was badly in need of a little kindness right then.

'Why don't you tell me all about it?' Miranda suggested softly.

Maybe if she'd eaten breakfast, or maybe if her body hadn't still been aching with the sweet memories of his lovemaking which now seemed to mock and wound her, then Catherine might have given a more thoughtful and considered response.

But memories of betrayal—her mother's and now

her own—fused into a blurred, salty haze before her eyes, and she nodded, biting her lips to prevent her voice from disintegrating into helpless sobs.

'Oh, Miranda!' she gulped. 'I've been so stupid.'

'Do you want to tell me what happened?'

She needed to tell *someone* about it. To unload her guilt. To make some kind of sense of it all. She shook her head. 'There's nothing to tell.'

'Try me.'

Distractedly, Catherine began voicing her thoughts out loud. 'Maybe it was a reaction to Peter—I *don't know*—I just know that I behaved in a way which was completely alien to me!'

'You slept with him?'

Catherine nodded. She supposed that was one way of putting it. 'Yes, I slept with him! I fell into his arms like the ripest plum on the tree. I spent the night with him. Me! *Me!* I still can't believe it!' Her voice rose in disbelief. 'I went out with Peter for three years and never even *looked* at another man.' But then, no man like Finn Delaney had come along for her to look at, had he? 'And before that there was only one significant other. I was too busy building up my career to be interested in men. And I've certainly never—*never*—been quite so free and easy. Not even with Peter.'

Especially not with Peter. Quite the opposite, in fact. Peter had been surprised that she had held out so long before letting them get intimate. He'd said it was a refreshing change to find a woman who played hard to get. But it hadn't been a game—it had been a necessity. Born out of a need for self-respect which her mother had drummed into her and a desire to have him respect *her*.

Which made her wonder what Finn Delaney must be thinking about her now.

'Maybe he has something special—this Finn Delaney.'

'Oh, he has something *special* all right!' burst out Catherine. 'Bucketfuls of charm and sex-appeal—and the ability to pitch it at just the right level to make himself irresistible to women!'

Miranda, not normally given to looking fazed, raised her eyebrows. 'That's some testimony, Catherine,' she murmured. 'I take it that he was a good lover?'

'The best,' said Catherine, before she had time to think about it. And with those two words she seemed to have managed to invalidate everything she had had with Peter, too. 'He was unbelievable.'

There was a long silence.

'You'll get over it,' said Miranda at last.

Catherine raised a defiant face, but her green eyes were full of a tell-tale glittering. 'I'll have to,' she said staunchly. 'I don't have any choice, do I?'

His face almost obscured by the creamy bloom of flowers and dark green foliage, Finn narrowed his eyes as he surveyed the names next to the doorbells.

Walker. Flat 3. He shifted the flowers onto one shoulder, as if he was winding a baby, and jammed his thumb on the bell.

Inside the flat, the bell pealed, and Catherine frowned, then stifled a small groan. Bad that someone should call unannounced after this week when she had lost almost everything. What had remained of her self-respect. Her pride. And now her job.

Miranda hadn't even had the grace to look ashamed

when Catherine had marched straight into her office and slammed the latest copy of *Pizazz!* on her desk.

'What the hell is *this* supposed to mean, Miranda?' she demanded.

Miranda's face was a picture of unconvincing innocence. 'You don't like the piece? I thought we did Dublin justice.'

'I'm not talking about the piece on Dublin and you know it, Miranda!'

'Yes.' Miranda's face turned into one of editorial defiance. 'The story was too good not to tell.'

'But there *was* no story, Miranda!' protested Catherine. 'You know there wasn't.' Except that there was. Of course there was. And it was the oldest trick in the journalist's book. Being creative with the facts.

The only facts that Miranda had gleaned from Catherine were that she had spent a wild night with Finn Delaney and that he had not asked to see her again. Miranda had discovered for herself that Catherine looked uncannily like an ex-lover of his, and from this had mushroomed a stomach-churningly awful piece all about Finn Delaney underneath Catherine's article on Dublin.

It described him as an 'unbelievable' lover, and hinted that his sexual appetite was as gargantuan as his appetite for success. It described the view from his bedroom in loving detail—and she didn't even remember telling Miranda about *that*! It did not actually come out and name Catherine as having been the recipient of his sexual favours, but it didn't need to. Catherine knew. And a few others had guessed.

But the person she had been astonished not to hear from was Finn Delaney—and she thanked God for the silence from that quarter, and the fact that *Pizazz!* didn't have a big circulation across the water.

'You deceived me, Miranda,' she told her editor quietly. 'You've threatened my journalistic integrity! I should bloody well go to the Press Complaints Commission—and so will Finn Delaney if he ever reads it and if he has an ounce of sense!'

'But it was in the public interest!' crowed Miranda triumphantly. 'A man who could be running a country—it's our *duty* to inform our readers what he's really like!'

'You don't have a clue what he's really like!' stormed Catherine. Though neither, in truth, did she. 'You've just succeeded in making him sound like some kind of vacuous stud with his brain stuffed down the front of his trousers!'

And with that Catherine had flung down her letter of resignation and stomped out of the office into an unknown future, her stomach sinking as she told herself that she could always go freelance.

The doorbell rang again.

Now, who the hell was bothering her at this hour in the morning? At nine o'clock on a Saturday morning most people were in bed, surely?

'Hello?' she said into the intercom, in a go-away kind of voice.

Downstairs, the petals of the scented flowers brushing against his cheek, Finn felt the slow build-up of tension. He had tried to pick a time when she would be in and it seemed that he had struck lucky.

His eyes glittered. He wanted to surprise her.

'Catherine?'

A maelstrom of emotions swirled around like a whirlpool in her befuddled brain as that single word instantly gave her the identity of her caller. But of course it would. She would recognise that rich Irish brogue from a hundred miles away, even if her guilty conscience hadn't been fighting a war with a suddenly stirring body.

Finn?

Finn?

Here?

He must have seen the article!

A fit of nerves assailed her. Catherine pressed her forehead against the door and closed her eyes. Oh, why the hell had she answered the wretched door in the first place? He knew now that she was here, and short of ignoring it and hoping he might go away...

She opened her eyes. Tried to imagine him shrugging those broad, powerful shoulders and just quietly leaving and failed miserably. She was trapped.

Presumably Finn Delaney had come here to wipe the floor with her. To tell her exactly what he thought of women who blabbed their tacky stories to middle-of-the-road magazines.

'Catherine?'

She tried to work out if he sounded furiously angry or just quietly seething, but the rich, lilting voice sounded nothing more than deeply irresistible.

'C-come up, Finn,' she suggested falteringly.

The words stayed in his mind as he rode up in the lift, and an odd sort of smile twisted his lips. Of course everything she said would drip with sexual innuendo—because it sure as hell was pretty much all they had really shared.

Sex.

But still he felt the unwilling burn of excitement just thinking about it.

Catherine had enough time to zip round her mouth with her electric toothbrush and then drag a comb through her long, mussed-up hair. The over-sized tee shirt which fell to an unflattering length at mid-knee she would just have to live with.

She cast a despairing glance in the mirror. At least she couldn't be accused of being a *femme fatale*.

Then her face paled as she heard the lift door open, and all flippancy fled as she remembered just why he was here. *Femme fatale,* indeed. As if he would look at her with anything but contempt after what had happened!

She opened the door before he had time to knock, and the first thing he thought was how pale her face looked without make-up. The second was that the baggy tee shirt did absolutely nothing to conceal the tight little buds of her nipples which thrust against the soft material. He felt himself harden.

'How lovely to see you!' she said brightly—which was true. Because he looked heart-stoppingly gorgeous in a pair of faded jeans and a sweater in a washed-out blue colour which made his eyes seem even more intense than usual. Her heart started crashing in her chest and she tensed in expectation, wondering how he was going to express himself.

Withering contempt? she wondered. Or blistering invective? But as she waited for the storm to rage over her, her pulse began to race in response to the confusing messages she was getting. He was carrying flowers. Strange, beautiful flowers, the like of which she had never seen before. With long white-green petals and dark leaves.

Flowers?

Finn gave a rueful shrug of his shoulders. 'Sorry.

It's a pretty unsociable hour to call, I know,' he murmured. 'And it looks like I just got you out of bed.'

She found herself blushing and hated herself for it. Why draw attention to a remembered intimacy which now seemed as false as a mirage? 'No, no—I've been awake for hours.' Which also was true; she certainly hadn't slept more than a couple of hours at a stretch since she had returned from her fateful trip to Dublin.

'Aren't you going to invite me in, Catherine?' His tone was as soft as the paw of a tiger moving stealthily through the jungle.

'You want to come in?' she questioned stupidly. Well, of course he did—no doubt a man of his status would object to a slanging match where the occupants of the nearby apartments were in danger of hearing!

He gave a half-smile. 'Is this how you usually react when lovers appear on your doorstep offering you flowers?'

He handed her the flowers but she barely registered their beauty—because all her attention had focused on that one hopeful word he had uttered.

Lovers.

That didn't sound past tense, did it? Which meant not one, but two things. That he couldn't possibly have read the article, and that possibly—just possibly—he wanted to carry on where they had left off in Ireland. But did *she*?

Of course she did! Just the sight of him was making her mind take flight into a flower-filled fantasy world where it was just her and Finn. Finn and her. Uttering a silent prayer of thanks, she swallowed down her excitement as she stared at the exotic blooms.

'They're for me?' she asked, even more stupidly.

He raised his eyebrows. 'Did you think I'd be so

insensitive as to turn up here carrying flowers for someone else?'

'I suppose not.' She smiled, hardly daring to acknowledge the growing pleasure which was slowly warming her blood, so that she felt as if she was standing in front of a roaring fire. 'Come in,' she said, and drew the door open. She thrust her nose into the forgotten blooms as the most delicious and beguiling scent filled her nostrils. 'These are absolutely gorgeous,' she breathed. 'Just gorgeous. And so unusual.' She turned wide green eyes to his. 'What are they?'

His voice was careless. 'Mock orange blossom.'

'You mean as opposed to real orange blossom?' she joked.

'Something like that.'

She'd never seen mock orange blossom on the stalls of her local flower market, but perhaps Finn Delaney had stopped to buy them in one of the more exclusive department stores. She smiled again, not bothering to hide her delight. 'I'll go and put them in water—please, make yourself at home.' Did that sound too keen? she wondered as she went off to the kitchen to find a vase.

Oh, who cared? Wasn't a man who turned up on your doorstep first thing on a Saturday morning bearing flowers being more than a little keen himself?

Maybe he felt the same as she did, deep down. That the time they had shared in Greece, and then in Dublin, hinted at a promise too good to just let go.

Humming happily beneath her breath, she filled a vase with water.

Finn prowled around the sitting room like a caged tiger, noting the decor with the eye of a man used to registering detail and analysing it.

The curtains were still drawn—soft gold things, through which the morning sun filtered, gilding the subdued light and giving the room a slightly surreal feel.

Lots of books, he noted. Run-of-the-mill furniture. Two fairly ordinary sofas transformed from the mundane by the addition of two exotic throws. A couple of framed prints and a collection of small china cats. Not enough to tell him anything much about the real Catherine Walker. His mouth flattened as she walked back into the room and deposited the flowers in the centre of a small pine coffee table. Their scent filled the room.

Now what? wondered Catherine. Were they going to carry on as if nothing had happened between them? 'Coffee?' she asked.

He shook his head and moved towards her, driven on by some primeval urge deep within him. His eyes were shuttered as he pulled her into his arms, feeling her soft flesh pliant against the hard lines of his body, which sprang into instant life in response. 'I haven't come here for coffee.'

She opened her mouth to protest that he might at least adhere to a *few* conventional social niceties before he moved in for the kill, but by then he had lowered his mouth onto hers, and she was so hungry for his kiss that she let him. How long had it been? Four weeks that felt like a lifetime…

'God, Finn—'

'What?' He cupped her breast with arrogant possession, liking the way that the nipple instantly reacted, pressing like a little rock against his hand.

To be in his arms once more was even better than she remembered, and the honeyed pleasure which was invading her senses was driving every thought out of her head other than the overriding one—which was how much she wanted this. Him.

'Mmm? You were saying?'

'W-was I? I can't remember.' Catherine's hands roved beneath the washed-out blue sweater, greedily alighting on the silken skin there. 'Oh, it's so good to see you.'

'And you, too. And this is certainly the kind of welcome I was hoping for.' His voice sounded thickened, slurred. He drew his mouth away from hers and his eyes were glittering with blue fire. 'My only objection is that I'm not seeing quite enough of you, Catherine. Don't you think it's time to remedy that situation?'

And with a single fluid movement he peeled the tee shirt off her body, over her head, and threw it to the ground, so that she was standing naked before him.

'Finn!' She felt the air cool her already heated body, but any consternation fled just as soon as he touched his lips to her nipple, and she began to shake as she clutched his dark head further against her breast. 'Oh, God!'

That shuddered cry of pure, undiluted desire fuelled his already overwhelming hunger, and he yanked his sweater over his head, kicked off his deck shoes, pulled roughly at the belt of his jeans and unzipped them. 'Take them off,' he commanded unsteadily.

On fire with her need for him, Catherine sank to her knees and slid the denim down over the hard, muscular shaft of his thighs, burying her head in the very cradle of his masculinity, her tongue flicking out to touch him where he was burningly hard. He groaned.

'Are you always like this?' he demanded, once the jeans were discarded, and he drew her down with an urgent need onto the carpet, their naked bodies colliding and merging with a mutual greed.

'Like what?' Hungrily she nipped at a hard brown nipple and he shuddered.

'So responsive.' So bloody easy to turn on, and so fiendishly good at turning *him* on until he thought he might explode with need.

Only with you, she thought, but that seemed too frighteningly vulnerable a thing to say. She licked instead.

He moved over her, his eyes burningly bright—a strange, shining combination of blue and black. In the heat of the moment his mind went blank and he forgot everything other than the sweet temptation of her flesh.

'God, Catherine, I want you so badly.' He slipped his hand between her thighs, where she was as wet as he had known she would be, and a wild kind of fever heated his blood. He moved and then groaned, then groaned again as he thrust into her, deep and hard and long, and she gave a low, exultant scream of pleasure.

'Is that good?' he ground out. 'Because—sweet God in heaven—it feels good to me!'

She gave herself up to the delicious rhythm, feeling control beginning to slip away.

'Is it, Catherine?' he urged, wanting to hear the surrender he could feel in her fast-shivering flesh. 'Is it good?'

Through dry lips she managed to say the very word

she had said to Miranda. 'Unbelievable,' she groaned, as he filled her and moved inside her. 'Unbelievable.'

It happened so quickly, and her orgasm seemed to make Catherine's world explode. For a moment consciousness actually receded, and she was lost in a dreamy, perfect world of feeling and sensation, then it slowly ebbed back and reality was just as good. She smiled. That was if reality was lying naked in Finn's arms with the whole day—maybe even the weekend—ahead of them.

And this time they would do things other than make love. She could cook him lunch—had she got enough food to produce something impressive?—and then afterwards she could take him to the park. Maybe an early film, and then supper... Sooner rather than later she was going to have to come clean about her job, and very probably the mix-up about the article, but she could deal with that. She was certain she could...

'Mmm,' she breathed in anticipation. *'Mmm!'*

Her ecstatic response shattered his equilibrium and a sudden icy chill shivered its way over his bare flesh.

Finn withdrew from her and rolled away, and the physical deprivation of his presence made her whimper like a lost little animal.

'What are you doing?' she murmured sleepily, watching through half-slitted eyes the graceful, muscular body as he reached for his jeans.

'What does it look like? I'm getting dressed.'

He pulled the jeans back on and zipped them up before replying, and suddenly his face was shuttered. This was a new, hard Finn she didn't recognise, with a new, hard voice she didn't recognise either.

'Wh-where are you going?'

'I don't think that's really any of your business, do you?'

Catherine screwed up her eyes as she sat up, thinking that she must have misheard him—or that perhaps she had slipped unknowingly into a nightmare made uncannily real by his expressionless face. 'What?'

The movement which curved his lips was a bitter parody of a smile. 'Shall I repeat it for you in words of one syllable, Catherine?' he questioned cruelly. 'I said it's none of your business. Got that?' And he slipped his feet into the deck shoes, jerked on the blue sweater.

Her mind was spinning as it strove to make sense of this bizarre ending to what had just happened. Perhaps if she wasn't so befuddled by the aftermath of her orgasm then she might have made sense of it sooner. 'Finn, I don't understand—'

'Oh, don't you?' His mouth twisted and the blue eyes were as cold as ice. 'Then you can't be very good at your job, can you? If you lack the ability to understand the implication behind a simple sentence like that!'

The penny dropped. Her job, he had said. Yes, of course. Her job—her wretched, wretched job! Oh, God—he *had* seen the article! 'Finn, I want to explain—'

'Oh, please—spare me your lies. Just don't *bother*!'

Realising that she was completely naked, Catherine grabbed at her tee shirt and wriggled it over her head as she scrambled to her feet, aware of the movement of her breasts and aware too that Finn wasn't oblivious to their movement either. She turned to him with a face full of appeal, and suddenly nothing was more important than establishing the truth. 'You owe me the right to explain what happened,' she said in a low voice.

'I owe you *nothing*!' he spat back, and the temper which had been simmering away came boiling over, words spilling out of his mouth without thought or care. 'In fact, quite the contrary—I felt that in view of the fact I'd been paid nothing for an article about me which *I did not agree to*, then I should take my payment *in kind*!'

It took a moment or two for the meaning behind his words to sink in, and when it did Catherine felt sick. Physically sick. And even worse was the look in his eyes...

So here was the look of blistering contempt she had been anticipating at the very beginning but had conveniently forgotten when he had given her flowers and put his arms around her. And it was even worse than in her most fevered imaginings...

She swallowed down the bitter taste in her mouth, barely able to believe what he was implying. 'Y-you mean...you mean...you came here today *deliberately* to have sex with me—'

'Sure,' he answered arrogantly. 'It wasn't difficult—but why should it be? It was as easy as pie the last time.'

She wanted to hit him, to shout, to scream at him— but still she forced herself to question him, because surely there was some kind of ghastly mistake. 'To get your own back for some stupid magazine article?' she finished faintly.

'"Some stupid magazine article"?' Two high lines of colour ran across his cheekbones, and his Irish accent seemed even more pronounced. 'It may be just some stupid article to you, sweetheart, but it has very effectively sent my credibility flying!'

'You mean that you wanted to look whiter than white because you hope to run for government?' she demanded.

'That has nothing to do with it!' His voice became a low hiss. 'Other people put labels on me that I do not seek for myself! I couldn't give a stuff about politics, but I *do* care what my friends and family read about me!'

And he fixed her with a look of such utter scorn that Catherine actually flinched.

Her own look matched his for scorn now. 'And the flowers? Such an elaborate masquerade, Finn,' she said bitterly. 'Did you really have to go to so much trouble to ensure my seduction? Did you think that your powers of persuasion were slipping?'

'I never doubted that for a minute, sweetheart,' he drawled, and then his eyes gleamed and his voice softened. 'No, the bouquet was to send you a silent message.'

She stared at him uncomprehendingly.

'Did you never hear of the language of flowers, Catherine?'

The question and the way he asked it were so close to the image of the poetic Irishman who had swept her off her feet that for a moment Catherine was lulled into imagining that the things he had said were not real.

She shook her head.

'Every flower carries its own message,' he continued softly.

'And the mock orange blossom?' she asked shakily. 'What does that stand for?'

'Can't you guess?' He paused, and raised his dark eyebrows. 'Not got it yet, Catherine? Deceit,' he said finally, with a cruel, hard smile.

She supposed that as a gesture it deserved some kind of accolade, but it felt like a knife being twisted over and over in her gut.

'Just tell me one thing,' he said, and his eyes were piercingly clear. 'When you came to Dublin did your editor send you? Was it just coincidence that brought you? Or did she tell you to get something on me?'

Catherine opened her mouth. 'Well, she told me to, yes. But—'

'But what? The article just wrote itself, did it?' he questioned witheringly.

She wanted to say, It wasn't like that! But she knew that no words in the dictionary could ever make things right between them now.

'Please go,' she said quietly.

But he was already by the door. 'Nothing would give me greater pleasure,' he grated.

And with that he was gone.

CHAPTER SEVEN

THE moment the door had shut behind him, Catherine snatched the flowers from out of the vase and took them to the kitchen sink, where she squashed them ruthlessly with a rolling pin, bashing and bashing at them until they were made pulp.

That should relieve some of her pent-up frustration, she thought, with a fleeting feeling of triumph which evaporated almost immediately. Except that she wasn't feeling frustrated—not in the physical sense, in any case. No, her frustration was born out of the random and cruel tricks of fate which had led her into this situation. The man whom she had fallen for, hook, line and sinker, would never trust her again.

But he didn't even give you a chance to explain yourself, she reminded herself bitterly—and in the heat of the moment she had forgotten to ask him about Deirdra O'Shea. Finn Delaney himself was no saint, she thought. And there had been a reason why she had been so indiscreet with Miranda.

Tears began to slide down her cheeks just as the telephone rang.

She snatched it up, despising herself for the eagerness which prompted her, thinking that maybe Finn had had a change of heart—was ringing her to apologise for his unbelievably cruel behaviour.

'H-hello?'

But it was her mother. 'Catherine? Are you all right?'

Catherine wiped the tears away with a bunched fist. 'Of course I'm all right, Mum.'

'Well, you don't sound it.' Her mother's voice sounded worried, but of course it would. Mothers were notoriously good at detecting when their daughters were crying, particularly when they were as close as Catherine and her mother. 'Have you been crying?'

'Not really.' Sniff.

'Not really?' Her mother's voice softened. 'Do you want to tell me about it?'

'I can't! You'll hate me for it!'

'Catherine, stop it. Tell me what's happened.'

Such was her distress that the story came tumbling out—or rather an edited version designed to cause the least hurt to her mother. Catherine did not mention that she barely knew the man, nor the shockingly short time scale involved. She just told her the simple truth of the matter, which was that she had leapt into a foolish and inconsidered relationship straight after Peter and that it was now over.

'Oh, Mum!' she wailed. 'How could I have done it?'

'You did it on the rebound,' her mother said firmly. 'Lots of people do. It isn't the end of the world! Just try to put it out of your mind and forget about it.'

'And I hadn't seen Peter for months and months!' Catherine found herself saying, which again was true. She didn't want her mother thinking that she was about to start taking lovers at the drop of a hat.

'I'm not making any value judgements, darling. I know the sort of person you are. I've never doubted you for a moment, and anyone who does needs their head examining!' she finished fiercely. 'Who is this man—is he married?'

Catherine heard the slightly raw tone. Even now her mother still hurt. She had had her own cross to bear. Loving a married man had brought with it nothing but pain and heartache. And a baby, of course. Mustn't forget the baby. For Catherine had been one of those fatherless children—a child who had never known her father. 'No, he's not married.'

'Thank God for that!'

'I shouldn't have worried you by telling you about it, Mum.'

'I'm more worried about the fact that you don't have a job any more,' her mother was saying. 'Any luck on the freelance front?'

'I haven't really been looking—'

'Well, better start, Catherine—you have to keep a roof over your head and food in your mouth and clothes on your back, remember?'

Oh, yes, she remembered all right. Independence had been another lesson drummed into her from an early age by a woman who had always had to fend for herself and bring up her child. Catherine's mother had initially been wary of her daughter's chosen career, seeing it as precarious—and for Catherine to now be freelance must be her idea of a nightmare.

'Oh, I'll find something—I've got plenty of contacts.'

'Why don't you come down this weekend? It'd be lovely to see you.'

Catherine hesitated, tempted. She couldn't think of anything nicer than to escape to her mother's tiny cottage, surrounded by fields and trees, with a distant peep of the sea. Under normal circumstances she would have been scooting straight out of the door to buy her ticket at the train station.

But these were not normal circumstances. No, indeed. Catherine cast a disgusted look down at her baggy tee shirt.

'No, Mum,' she replied. 'I have a heap of things to do here. Maybe next weekend.'

'All right, darling. You will take care of yourself, won't you?'

'Of course I will!'

Her mother's words came back to haunt her during the next few weeks as Catherine scouted around many publications angling for assignments. She had a mixed bag of luck. Some people knew her work and respected it, and were keen to hire her. But the market was full of freelance journalists—some of them talented and hungry and straight out of college—and Catherine knew that she was going to have to work very hard to keep up with the competition. Suddenly the staff job she had had at *Pizazz!* seemed terribly comfortable, and she wondered why she had bothered throwing it in.

As a defiant gesture it had been rather wasted. She had lost Finn anyway—though she reminded herself that he had never been hers to have.

And what else had her mother said?

'Take care of yourself.'

Had she known that the stress of everything that had happened would leave Catherine feeling distinctly peaky?

Stress had all kinds of insidious effects on the human body, she knew that as well as the next person. It played havoc with her appetite, for example. One minute she would be feeling so nauseous that just the thought of food would make her feel sick. The next she would be diving for the biscuit tin and thickly spreading yeast extract on a pile of digestive biscuits.

It wasn't until one afternoon when Sally—her best friend on *Pizazz!* and the only person she had kept in touch with from there—commented that she was putting on weight that Catherine's safe reality finally crumbled into dust.

She waited until Sally had gone and then shut the door behind her with a shaking hand. She went into the bathroom to stare at her white, haunted face with frightened eyes. Knowing deep down and yet denying it. Not wanting to know, nor daring to.

The thought that she might be pregnant simply hadn't occurred to her. But as she allowed the facts to assemble logically in her head she wondered how she could have been so stupid.

The next day she went through the rituals of confirmation, knowing that they were unnecessary, but until concrete proof confirmed her worst fears she might really be able to put it down to stress.

The blue line on the indicator was a fact. Just as was the faint tingling in her breasts. The missed periods. The nausea. The compulsive and compensatory eating. It all added up—and you wouldn't need to be Doctor of the Year to work out why.

Catherine sat back on her heels and took a deep breath, hugged her arms protectively around her heavy breasts.

Now what?

Her breathing short and shallow and low, she tried to flick her mind through her options. But nothing she thought of seemed to make any sense because it didn't seem real. It couldn't be real, could it?

She went into denial. Threw her energy into an

article on pet cemeteries and spent days researching it. Managed to agree to an almighty fee for a piece on London's newest wannabe club and spent a queasy evening in a smoke-filled room regretting it.

She denied it all over Christmas by wearing baggy jumpers and telling her bemused mother that she was trying to 'cut down' when asked why she wasn't drinking.

And still the days ticked by—until one morning, after dashing to the bathroom to be sick, she gripped the washbasin with still-shaking hands and stared at her white-green reflection in the mirror.

She was pregnant with Finn Delaney's baby!

A man who despised her, a man she barely knew—a man, moreover, who had walked out of her life with the clear wish of never setting eyes on her again.

She was going to have a baby.

And with that one focused thought all her options and choices dissolved into one unassailable fact.

She was going to have a baby.

She booked an appointment with her doctor, who raised her eyebrows questioningly at Catherine when she'd finished her examination.

'Yes, you're pregnant, though you're fine—fit and healthy.' The doctor frowned. 'You really should have come to see me sooner, you know.'

'Yes, I know.'

The doctor appeared to choose her words delicately. 'And you're going to go ahead with the pregnancy? Because if you're not…'

Catherine didn't even have to think about it. Some things you just knew, with a bone-deep certainty. She drew a deep breath, scared yet sure. Very, very sure. 'Oh, yes. Very definitely.'

The doctor nodded. 'How about the father? Will he be able to support you?'

Another pause. There was no doubt that he would be *able* to. But… 'I'm not expecting him to. We're not…together any more.' How was that for managing to make the truth sound respectable?

'But you'll tell him?'

Catherine sat back in her chair. 'I don't know.' She didn't feel she knew anything any more.

The doctor straightened the papers on her desk and looked at her. 'A man has a right to know, Catherine—I really believe that.'

Catherine walked back to her flat, scarcely noticing the light drizzle which slowly seeped into her skin and clothes. The doctor's question refused to go away. *Should* she tell him? Did he really have a right to know that he had fathered a baby?

She sat in the sitting room, nursing a cup of tea which grew cold and unnoticed, while the floor where she and Finn had made love seemed to mock her nearly as much as her idealistic thoughts.

Made love, indeed!

She might have been swept away with the passion of seeing him again, but Finn's seduction had been cold-blooded in thought, if not in deed.

And yet the responsibility was just as much his as hers, surely?

She could be proud and vow never to tell him that his child was growing inside her womb, but what of the child itself?

Was she going to subject him or her to a lifetime of what she had had to endure? The terrible insecurity of not knowing who your father was? Of growing up with one vital half of the gene jigsaw missing? And with her having to nurse some terrible, pointless secret?

So did she pick up the telephone and tell him? Or write him a letter detailing the consequences of their moment of madness? She winced as she attempted to compose a clumsy paragraph inside her head. Impossible.

The sun began to dip in the sky and she put the cup of untouched tea down on the coffee table as tears began to slide down her cheeks. She angrily brushed them away, her heart aching for the new life inside her. Why should her baby suffer just because two adults had acted without thought?

She needed courage, more courage than she had ever needed before, because there was only one way to tell him something like this.

Face to face.

CHAPTER EIGHT

'I'M SENDING Miss Walker through, Finn.'

'Thanks, Sandra.' Finn flicked off the intercom and waited, sitting very still behind the huge desk as the door to his office opened and Catherine walked in, an indefinable expression in her green eyes. She wore a black velvet coat—a loose, swingy sort of thing—and with its contrast against her pale face and black hair she looked liked a beautiful sorceress.

'Come in, Catherine,' he said evenly, and rose to his feet. 'Shut the door behind you.'

As if she needed telling! As if she wanted his assistant to hear what she was about to say to him—and the ensuing discussion which would inevitably follow it. She shut it.

'Sit down, won't you?' He sat down himself and gestured to the chair opposite his, but Catherine shook her head.

'I'll stand, if you don't mind. I've been cooped up on a flight and in a cab,' she said. And although she knew that the flutterings in her stomach were due to nerves, and not the baby, she wasn't going to risk sitting in front of him and squirming. She met his gaze. 'I'm surprised that you agreed to see me.'

'I'm surprised that you want to.'

In his unmoving face only his blue eyes showed signs of life. His features looked as cold and as motionless as if they had been hewn from rock as old as the stone of Glendalough, where he had taken her that day which now seemed an age ago. And it was. It had been a different Catherine who looked up and laughed into his eyes that day.

The Catherine who was here was on a mission. To give him the truth—a truth which she felt honour-bound to tell him. But wasn't it funny how you could practise saying something over and over again, yet when the opportunity came the words just wouldn't seem to come?

Finn watched her as he waited, thinking that some-how she looked different—and not just because her face was closed and wary and pale. No, there was something he couldn't quite put his finger on, some-thing which alerted his sixth sense. The same sense which told him that a beautiful woman like Catherine Walker must have her pride. A pride which would have no time for a man who had acted as he had done. Yet she had phoned asking to speak to him. Person-ally and urgently.

'I'm all yours, Catherine,' he said, and then wished he hadn't, for the irony hadn't escaped him—nor her either, to judge from her brief, bitter smile.

No need to preface it with anything as humiliating as, Do you remember when we last met in London...? Such a distortion of the truth would only embarrass them.

'I'm pregnant,' she said baldly.

There was a long, long silence, but not a flicker of emotion crossed his face. 'I see.'

'It's yours!' she declared wildly, wanting to shatter the tense expectation in the air, to breathe some life into that unmoving face of his.

'Yes.'

Catherine stared at him, and delayed shock, together with his cold and monosyllabic reply, made her legs feel like water. She sank into the chair he had originally offered and stared at him with wide, uncomprehending eyes.

'You aren't going to deny it?'

'What would be the point? I can't imagine that I would be your first choice as father to your child. What we had between us hardly qualifies as the greatest love affair of all time, does it? So why would you lie about something as important as that? And if you aren't lying then the logical conclusion is that you must be telling the truth.'

It was a cold and analytical assessment and, oddly enough, seemed to hurt far more than if he had just lost his temper and flatly denied it—called her all names under the sun and told her to get out of his office and his life. For a start, it would have given her a let-out clause.

And it would have shown passion. Feelings. *Something* other than this cold and distant look in his eyes. As if he were a scientist surveying some rather odd-looking specimen in a test-tube. But then, what had she expected? 'You don't seem surprised,' she said heavily.

He shrugged. 'A simple case of cause and effect.'

'How very cynical, Finn.'

'Cynical, but true,' he mocked, then drew a deep breath as he thought back to that mad and tempestuous morning in her London flat. He gave a long and heavy sigh. 'That's what comes of forgetting to wear a condom, I suppose.'

Reduced to the lowest possible denominator.

Catherine flinched, as though he had hit her. And he might as well have hit her, the pain in her heart was so intense. She remembered the frantic way they had fallen to the floor, the wild hunger she had felt for him, and he, apparently, for her.

Yet he had come there that day with just such a seduction—if such a word could be used to describe something so basic—in mind. But he had not protected himself, and she had been too caught up in the mood and the magic—yes, magic—to notice.

She could deny it until she was blue in the face, but Finn Delaney had completely had her in his thrall. Then, and before. But now she saw the so-called magic for what it was—an illusion—like a trick of the light.

'Was your lack of care simply an omission on your part?' she questioned.

'What do you think?' he demanded. 'That I did it deliberately? That I somehow hoped for this particular little scenario?' His blue gaze bored into her. 'What was I *thinking*?' He gave a low, bitter laugh. 'That's the trouble, you see, Catherine—I wanted you so badly that I wasn't thinking at all.'

'A wanting fuelled by contempt,' she observed bitterly, noticing that he didn't deny it.

'And when is the—?'

His deep, musical Irish voice faltered just a little.

He stared down at the figures he had been working on, and she noticed that it was the first time he had let any emotion creep in.

He looked up again. 'When is the baby due?'

'They aren't sure.'

The blue gaze became more intense. Quizzical. Silently demanding some kind of explanation. And of course he was entitled to one. She was here, wasn't she? She had foisted paternity on him and with that he had earned certain entitlements.

'I wasn't really sure about my dates myself, that's all. June—they think.'

'June.' He stared unseeingly out at the panoramic view from the window. 'So I'm to be a father some time in June?'

'Not necessarily.'

Now it was *his* turn to flinch, the dark-featured face looking both pained and quietly thunderous, and she realised that he had grossly misinterpreted her words.

'No, no, no!' she defended instantly. 'I didn't mean *that*. What I mean is that you don't have to have anything to do with this baby. Not if you don't want to.' He had not sought fatherhood, and therefore he should not be shackled by it.

'So why exactly are you here, Catherine?' He narrowed his eyes at her thoughtfully. 'Is it money you want?'

His mercenary judgement was like a slap to the face, and Catherine blanched as she shakily tried to rise to her feet. But there seemed to be no power to her legs. How much more hurt could he inflict on her?

'How dare you say that?' she hissed with an angry pride. 'You may be a big, powerful, rich businessman, but if you think I've come here today begging—*begging* for your largesse,' she repeated on a shuddering breath, 'then you are very much mistaken, Finn Delaney!'

'So just what *do* you want? A ring on your finger?'

'Hardly!' she contradicted witheringly. 'Strange as it may seem, I have no desire to tie myself to a man who thinks so badly of me that he believes I would treat my child as a commodity! Actually, I came here today to tell you about the baby simply because I felt that as an intelligent human being you would want to accept your share of responsibility for what has happened.'

'Catherine—'

'No!' Anger was giving her strength—beautiful, restorative strength. 'You've made your views perfectly clear. Don't worry, I won't be troubling you again!'

'I guess you could always sell your story to the highest bidder,' he said consideringly, and then ducked instinctively as something whizzed across the room.

Catherine had picked up the nearest object to her on his desk, which happened to be a large and very heavy paperweight, and it flew a foot wide of him and bounced deafeningly against the wall, bringing a marvellous landscape painting shattering down beside it, the glass breaking into a million shards.

The office door flew open and Sandra, his assistant, ran in, her eyes taking in the scene in front of her with disbelief. 'Oh, my God! Is everything all right, Finn?' she asked, her soft Irish accent rising in alarm. 'Would you have me call Security?' She stared at a white-faced and mutinous Catherine. 'Or the police?'

But Finn, astonishingly, was laughing—a low, gravelly laugh.

He shook his head. 'No, no—leave it, Sandra,' he said. 'Everything's fine. Miss Walker was just getting in a bit of target practice!'

'But unfortunately I missed!' said Catherine, her voice tinged with a slight hysteria. Her chair scraped back as she struggled to her feet.

'That will be all, thanks, Sandra,' said Finn quickly.

Sandra gave him one last, mystified stare before exiting the room and shutting the door behind her, just as Catherine reached it.

But Finn was quicker, beside her in a moment, where he caught hold of her shoulder. 'You're not going anywhere!'

'Let go of me!'

'No.' He moved her away from the door and whirled her round. He could see that she was very, very angry indeed. 'You could have killed me, you know,' he observed slowly.

'I wasn't aiming at you!' she snapped. 'But I wish to God I had!'

'What, and leave your child without a father?'

'You're not fit to be a father!'

He saw how distressingly white her face was and his whole manner altered. No matter what his feelings on the subject, the fact remained that she was pregnant. With his baby. And this kind of scene could surely not be doing her any good.

'Come and sit down and have some tea.'

'I don't want any tea! I want to go home!'

'To London? I think not. You're in no fit state to be flying back today. Not in your condition.'

It was that time-honoured phrase which did it. Which finally broke down the barriers she had tried to erect around her heart. *In your condition.* Someone should have been saying that to her with tender loving care. Preferably a husband who adored her, worshipped the ground she walked on, wanted to rub the small of her back and wait on her. Not a man who had had sex with her as some primitive kind of revenge and got so carried away with himself that he hadn't stopped to think about the consequences.

Though neither had she.

And instead she was about to replicate exactly what she had spent her whole life vowing not to do. Becoming a single mother, with all the emotional and financial hardship which went with that role.

She thought back to her own childhood. Her mother doing two and sometimes three jobs to make ends meet, so that Catherine should never feel different from the other children. Of course, she *had* felt different—some of the other children had made sure of that—but she had always been fed and clothed and loved and warm enough.

She had prayed that her mother would meet someone, but when eventually she had he had regarded Catherine as an encumbrance. Someone who was in the way and would always be in the way of his new wife and himself. He hadn't been outwardly horrible to her, but she had seen the hostility in his eyes sometimes, and it had frightened her.

Her mother must have seen it, too—for one day she had greeted Catherine at the school gates, a little pale and a little trembling, and told her that she was no longer going to marry Johnny. Catherine had laughed with delight and hugged her mother, and they had gone out and eaten tea and scones in a small café. His name had never been mentioned again.

How often had she hoped to repay her mother for her hard work and sacrifice by providing lavishly for her as she became older? Hadn't she dreamed of being one of the most snapped-up journalists in the land? Of maybe one day even writing a novel—a novel which would be a bestseller, naturally. She would buy her mother's cottage for her, make her old age secure.

Instead of which she must now go and destroy her mother's hopes and dreams for her. And her own, too.

She wanted to go away and just howl in some dark and private corner, but she saw that Finn was effectively barring the door.

'Are you going to let me leave?'

'What do you think?'

She fixed him with an icy look. 'I could scream the place down—that would get ''Security'' up here in a flash—if they thought you were raping me!'

He opened his mouth to say something, but thought better of it. Now was not the time to make a cheap and clever remark. 'Sit down, Catherine.'

'No, I w-won't.'

'Sit *down*, will you, woman? Or do I have to pick you up and carry you?'

It was like a brand-new sapling trying to withstand the full force of a hurricane. Catherine gave a weary sigh. She could see that he meant business, and besides, sitting down was what she wanted to do more than anything else in the world. Though lying down would have been better. Much better.

She sat down in the chair and closed her eyes. 'Go away,' she mumbled. 'Leave me alone.'

'Your logic is failing you,' he said drily. 'This is *my* office, remember.' He flicked on the intercom again. 'Sandra, will you have us sent in some tea? Good, strong tea. Oh, and something to eat?'

'Cake, Finn? Your favourite chocolate?' purred Sandra.

'Something more substantial than cake,' he replied, with a swift, assessing look at Catherine's fined-down cheekbones. 'A big, thick sandwich with a bit of protein in the middle.'

'Did you not have your lunch, Finn?' giggled Sandra.

'*Now*, please, Sandra!' he snapped.

'Why, *certainly*!' his assistant replied, in a hurt and huffy voice.

His face was stern as he looked down at Catherine, who was still sitting in the chair with her eyes closed. 'Are you asleep?' he asked quietly.

'No. Just trying to block out the sight of your face!'

'And what if the baby looks like me?' he questioned. 'Won't that be a terrible problem?'

Catherine opened her eyes and steeled herself against the impact of his handsome, mocking features. 'I hope it's a girl,' she said frostily. 'Who looks as little like you as possible! And even if he or she *does* look like you—'

'Yes?'

'I'll still love them!' she declared fiercely. 'I may not have a lot to offer, but I can give this baby love, Finn Delaney! Now, are you please going to let me go? Or am I a prisoner here?'

He spoke using the soothing voice of a psychiatrist who was trying to placate an extremely mad patient. 'You're not going anywhere until you've calmed down.'

'Then get me as far away from you as possible— that's the only way to guarantee *that*!'

There was a light tap on the door. 'Come in, Sandra,' called Finn rather drily, noting how circumstances could change routine. Sandra never, ever knocked. But then he never, ever had women turning up at his headquarters hurling paperweights against the wall!

A frosty-looking Sandra deposited a loaded tray on the low table in one corner of the room.

'Will there be anything else, Finn?'

He shook his head. 'No—thanks, Sandra.'

'You're welcome.'

He couldn't miss the trace of sarcasm, but then maybe it wasn't so very surprising. Sandra had been with him for years, had seen him run his affairs with cool-headed acumen and detachment.

'Catherine?'

'What?'

'Do you take sugar?'

She almost laughed aloud at the irony of it all—until she remembered that it wasn't in the least bit funny. Her green eyes blazed with a kind of furious indignation, directed at him, but felt deeply by herself.

'What a funny old world it is, don't you think, Finn? Here I am carrying your baby, and you don't even know whether I take sugar in my tea! Or milk, either, for that matter!' she finished wildly, wondering if she could put these sudden, violent mood swings down to fluctuating hormones. Or the bizarre situation she found herself in.

'So, do you or don't you?' he questioned calmly. 'Have sugar?'

'Usually I don't, no! But for now I'll have two!' she declared, experiencing a sudden desire for hot, sweet tea. 'And milk. Lots of it.'

He poured the tea and handed her a hefty-looking sandwich.

'I don't want anything to eat.'

'Suit yourself.'

But the bread and the ham looked mouthwateringly

good, and Catherine remembered that she had eaten nothing since a midnight craving had sent her to the fruit bowl last night and she had demolished the last three remaining apples. Her stomach rumbled and her hand reached out for the sandwich. She began to eat, looking at him defiantly, daring him to say something. But to his credit he simply took his own tea and sat down in front of her.

He waited until she had finished, relieved to see that the food and drink had brought a little colour into her cheeks. 'So now what? Where do we go from here?'

'I told you—I'm going back to London.'

He shook his head. 'I don't think so,' he demurred. 'You can't just arrive on my doorstep like the good fairy, impart a momentous piece of news like that, then take off again.'

'You can't stop me!'

'No, I can't stop you. But you still haven't told me why you came here today.'

'I would have thought that was pretty obvious.'

'Not really. You could have phoned me. Or written me a letter.' The blue eyes challenged her. 'So why didn't you?'

What was the point of hiding anything now? If she hadn't kept her job secret then he probably wouldn't have given her his card, and she wouldn't have gone to see him, and then this would never…

But she shook her head. What was the point of wasting time by thinking of what might have been? Or what might *not* have been, in this case.

'I wasn't sure that you'd believe me.'

'You thought that seeing me in person would convince me?' He frowned. 'But why? You don't *look* pregnant—' With that she opened the buttons of her coat and stared at him defiantly. He stilled.

For there, giving a smooth contour to her slim body, was the curve of pregnancy, and Finn stared at it, utterly speechless.

'I just knew I had to tell you face to face, and show you that it's real, it's happening,' she said, meeting that shocked stare. 'Besides, it isn't the easiest thing in the world to write, is it?'

He forced himself to remember that she had betrayed him. 'Even for a journalist?' he questioned sarcastically.

'Even for a journalist,' she echoed, but she felt the prick of tears at the back of her eyes and bit her lip again, knowing that whatever happened he had to hear *this* truth, too. He might not believe her, but she had to tell him.

'Finn, my editor *did* send me to Dublin when she found out we'd met—and she *did* try to get a story on you. But I said no.'

'So the story was just a figment of my imagination?' he queried sarcastically.

'No, but I didn't write that piece about you, and neither did I receive any money.'

'Oh?' he queried cynically. 'So they just happened to guess what the inside of my apartment is like, did they? And the fact that you obviously rate me in bed?'

'I was upset, and I blurted a few things out to my editor, not expecting her to use them.'

'What very naive behaviour for a journalist,' he said coldly, but his heart had begun to beat very fast. If she had been tricked into giving a confidence, then didn't that put an entirely different complexion on

matters? And didn't that, by default, make his sub-
sequent behaviour absolutely intolerable?

'Oh, what's the point in all this?' she sighed.
'Don't worry about it, Finn. I'm not asking you to
have anything to do with this baby.'

'But it's not just down to *you*, is it?' he asked quietly.

A cloud of apprehension cast its shadow. 'What do
you mean?'

'Just that I want to,' he said grimly. 'This is my
baby, too, you know, Catherine. By choosing to tell
me you have irrevocably involved me—and believe
me, sweetheart, I *intend* to be involved!

CHAPTER NINE

CATHERINE stared at Finn in shock and alarm.

'Well, what did you expect?' he demanded. 'That I would say, Okay—fine—you're having my baby? Here's a cheque and goodbye?'

'I told you—I did *not* come here asking you for money!' she said furiously.

'No? But you still haven't told me why you *did* come here.'

Catherine stared down at her lap, then looked back up at him, her eyes bright. 'Because I didn't know my own father.'

There was an odd, brittle kind of pause. 'You mean he died?' he questioned slowly.

She shook her head, met his eyes squarely. Defiantly. 'I'm illegitimate, Finn.'

'Come on now, Catherine,' he said gently. 'That isn't such a terrible thing to be.'

'Maybe not today it isn't—but things were different when I was a child.'

'Did you never meet him?'

'Never. I don't know whether he's alive or dead,' she said simply. 'He was married to someone, and it wasn't my mother. Like I said, I didn't know him and he didn't want to know me.' Her eyes were bright now. 'And I didn't want to inflict that on my own child.'

He caught a sense of the rejection she must have

felt, and again was filled with a pang of remorse. 'I'm sorry—'

'No!' Fierce pride made her bunch her fists to wipe away the first tell-tale sign of tears, and she set her shoulders back. 'I don't want or need your sympathy for my upbringing, Finn, because it was a perfectly happy upbringing. It's just—'

'Not for your childhood,' he said heavily. 'For my recklessness.'

Their eyes met. 'You don't have the monopoly on recklessness,' she said quietly. 'The difference is that our motivations were different. You came round hell-bent on revenge, and you extracted it in the most basic form possible, didn't you?'

Had he? Had he really been that cold-blooded? It was surely no defence to say that all he had planned to do was to deliver the flowers with a blistering de-nouncement, but that all rational thought and reason had been driven clean out of his mind by the sight and the touch and the feel of her. Was that the truth, or just a way of making events more palatable for his conscience?

'You have a very powerful effect on me, Catherine,' he said unsteadily. Because even now, God forgive him—even with all this going on—he was thinking that she looked like some kind of ex-quisite domesticated witch, with that tumble of ebony hair and the wide-spaced green eyes. Or a cat, he thought thickly. A minxy little feline who could sin-uously make him do her will.

What kind of child would they produce together? he found himself wondering. An ebony-haired child with passion running deep in its veins? 'A very pow-erful effect,' he finished, and met her eyes.

She steeled herself against his charm, the soft, sizzling look in his eyes. 'Yes, and we all know why, don't we? Why I have such an effect on you.'

His eyes narrowed. 'You're attempting to define chemistry?'

'I'm not defining anything—I'm describing something else entirely.' She threw him a challenging look and he matched it with one of his own.

'Go on,' he said. 'I'm intrigued.'

'We both know why such a famously private man should act in such an injudicious way.'

That one word assumed dominance inside his head. It wasn't a handle which had ever been applied to him before. 'Injudicious?'

'Well, wasn't it? If you'd bothered to find out a little bit more about me then you would have discovered that I was a journalist and presumably would have run in the opposite direction.'

'You were being deliberately evasive, Catherine. You know you were.'

'Yes, I was. I always am about my job, because people hold such strong prejudices.'

'Can you wonder why?' he questioned sarcastically.

'But it all happened so quickly—there was no time for an extended getting-to-know-you, was there, Finn? Tell me, do you normally leap into bed quite so quickly?'

'Not at all,' he countered, fixing her with a mocking blue look. 'Do you?'

'Never.' She drew a deep breath, not caring whether he believed her or not. His moral opinion of her did not matter. He would learn soon enough that she intended to be the mother to end all mothers. 'But maybe you didn't *need* to get to know me.'

'Now you've lost me.'

'Have I? Well, then, let me spell it out for you! We both know that the reason you couldn't wait to take me to bed was because I reminded you of your childhood sweetheart!'

'My childhood sweetheart?' he repeated incredulously.

'Deidra O'Shea! Are you denying that I look like her?'

It took a moment for her words to register, and when they did his accompanying feeling of rage was tempered only by the reminder that she was pregnant.

'You have a look of her about you,' he said carefully. 'But so what?'

'So *what*?' Catherine turned a furious face to him. 'Don't you realise how insulting that is for a woman?'

'What? That I happen to be attracted to dark-haired women with green eyes? Where's the crime in that, Catherine? Don't you normally lust after men who look like me? Isn't that what human nature is all about? That we're conditioned to respond to certain stimuli?'

What would it reveal about her if she admitted that she didn't usually lust after men at all? That Peter had been the very opposite of Finn in looks and character. Peter didn't dominate a room, nor did his charisma light it up just as surely as if it had been some glorious, glowing beacon. Peter had not been able to make her melt so instantly and so responsively with just a glimmering look from his eyes.

'Did you pretend I was her?' she demanded heatedly. 'Close your eyes and think it was her?'

'But I didn't close my eyes, Catherine,' he answered seriously. 'I was looking at you all the time. Remember?'

Oh, yes, she remembered. She remembered all too well. The way his eyes had caressed her just as surely as his fingertips had. The things he had said about her body. He had compared her skin to silk and cream, in that musical and lilting Irish accent.

'And what about you?' he questioned suddenly. 'What's the justification for your behaviour? Was it perhaps a way of striking out at a man who had hurt you badly?'

Her mouth opened, but no sound came out.

'Peter,' he said deliberately. 'The man who left you.'

'How on earth did you find out about Peter?' she breathed.

'Oh, come on, Catherine! When the article was brought to my attention by my cuttings service, I had a check run on you. Suddenly everything made sense. Why a woman, seemingly so aloof, should go to bed with me without me really having to try. You wanted to get back at your ex-boyfriend, didn't you?'

She let him believe it. Because the truth was even more disturbing than his accusation. That she had been so besotted by Finn she had scarcely given Peter a thought. Didn't that fact damn her more than redeem her?

Catherine felt tired. Weary. Unable to cope with any more.

'Oh, what's the point in remembering? What's done is done and we just have to live with the consequences.'

'Don't go back to London today,' he said suddenly.

She looked at him. 'Can you give me a good reason why not?'

'You're tired. And we have things to discuss.' His blue eyes gleamed with resolve, and he continued in a quieter voice, 'Just as there are consequences to what happened between us, there are also consequences to your visit here. Come on.' He stood up. 'Let's go.'

'Go where?'

'I'll take you back to the flat. You can rest there, and then we can talk.'

It wasn't so much his strength or his determination which made Catherine weakly nod her head. She was pregnant, she told herself. She was allowed to be persuaded.

'Okay,' she agreed.

Finn stared out of the window at the distant waters of the Liffey—grey today, to match the sky. And to match his mood, he thought, with a heart which was heavy.

He turned silently to look at where Catherine lay, asleep on the king-sized sofa. She had been fighting sleep ever since he had brought her back here and at long last she had given up the battle.

Her hair lay in tousled silken strands of black, contrasted against a Chinese silk cushion, and her dark lashes feathered into two perfect arcs on her high cheekbones. She slept as peacefully and as innocently as a child, he thought. He stared at the curve of her belly as his thoughts repeated themselves in his mind.

A child.

A wild leap of something like joy jumped unexpectedly in his chest.

A child!

And not just any child. This was *his* child.

And, no matter what the circumstances, wasn't the procreation of life always a miracle? Didn't the tiny heart of his child beat inside this woman?

This stranger.

And yet he felt he knew her body more intimately than that of any woman who had gone before.

Catherine opened her eyes to find Finn standing, staring down at her. For a moment she was muddled and confused, wondering just where she was and what had happened. And then it all came back to her in one great jolting rush.

She was in his flat, and she had told him, and his reaction had been—unexpectedly—one of immediate acceptance, not suspicion.

She sat up and yawned. 'I fell asleep,' she said unnecessarily.

'You certainly did.' He glanced at his watch. 'For almost an hour. Looked like you needed it.'

An hour! 'Good grief.' She yawned again. When was the last time she'd slept so soundly in the middle of the day? Better start getting used to changes, she thought, as she ran her hand through her rumpled hair. She looked up into the imposing, impassive face. 'What are we going to do?'

He gave an almost imperceptible nod. *We*, she had said, acknowledging the power in a single word. He realised that already they were a unit. If you were lovers, even married, then no matter how long you were in a relationship a certain question-mark of impermanence always hovered unspoken in the air. But not any more. He and Catherine were fact. Chained together for the rest of their lives. The mother, the father and the baby.

'Tell me about what your life in London is like,' he said suddenly, and seated himself on the sofa opposite hers, stretching his long legs out in front of him.

Catherine blinked. 'Like what? You know where I live.'

'Yes. A one-bedroomed flat in the middle of the city. Not the most ideal place for bringing up a baby,' he observed.

She was intelligent enough not to argue with that. 'No,' she agreed quietly. 'It's not.'

'And your job?' he questioned. 'On *Pizazz!*.' He spat the word out as though it was a bitter pill. 'Will they give you paid maternity leave?'

Catherine hesitated. Of course. He didn't know— but then how would he? 'I don't have a job any more,' she said slowly, and saw his head jerk upwards in surprise. 'Or rather, I do, but it's certainly not one which will give me paid maternity leave. I'm...I've gone freelance,' she said at last.

'Since when?' he demanded. 'Since before you knew you were pregnant?'

'Of course! I'm not *completely* stupid!'

Guilt twisted a knife in his gut. 'You can't get another staff job?'

'Not like this! Who's going to take someone on at this stage of pregnancy? I can just see it now—Welcome, Catherine, we'd love to employ you. And, yes, we'd be delighted to give you paid leave in a few months' time!'

He studied her, trying to be dispassionate, to block out her blinding beauty. 'So how exactly are you planning to bring up this baby, in Clerkenwell, with no regular income?'

'I haven't decided.'

'You make it sound as though you have the luxury of choice, Catherine—which it seems to me you don't.'

'I'll think of something.' Her mother had managed, hadn't she? Well, *so would she*!

He looked at her closely, this beautiful woman he had been unable to resist, recognising that their lives would never be the same again.

'Where does your mother live?' he questioned, so uncannily that for one mad moment she wondered if he was capable of reading her thoughts.

'Devon.'

'Would you consider going there?'

Catherine shuddered. What, and let the village watch history repeating itself? The conquering daughter returning home vanquished, pregnant, and trying to eke out a living? Could she possibly land herself on her mother—who was happy with her independent life and her charity work? Would she want to go through the whole thing yet again?

'It would be too much for my mother to cope with,' she said truthfully.

That was one option dealt with. 'And do you know many people in London?'

She shrugged. 'Kind of—though I've only been there a couple of years. Colleagues, of course. Well, ex-colleagues, mainly,' she amended. And work friendships were never the same once you'd left a job, were they? Everyone knew that. 'I've got some good close friends, too.'

'Any with children?'

'Good grief—no! Career women to a fault.'

'Sounds a pretty isolated and lonely place for a woman to be child-rearing.'

'Like I said, I'll manage.'

His eyes narrowed. 'Commendable pride, Catherine,' he said drily. 'But it isn't just you to think about now, is it? Do you really think it's fair to foist that kind of lifestyle on a poor, defenceless baby?'

'You're making it sound like cruelty!' she protested. 'Lots and lots of women have babies in cities and all of them are perfectly happy!'

'Most probably have supporting partners and extended families!' he snapped. 'Which you don't!'

'Well—'

'And most do not have a credible alternative,' he said, cutting right across her protests. 'Like you do,' he finished deliberately.

There was something so solemn and profound in his voice that Catherine instinctively sat up straight, half-fearful and half-hopeful of what his next words might be. 'Like what?' she whispered.

'You could come and live here, in Dublin.'

She stared at him as if he had suddenly sprouted horns. 'Are you out of your mind?'

'I don't think that my thinking could be described as normal, no. Though that's hardly surprising, given the topic,' he answered drily. 'But it's certainly rational. Consider it,' he said, seeing her begin to mouth another protest.

'I have, and it took me all of three seconds to reject it!' she answered crossly, despising the sudden rapid race in her heart-rate.

'Listen,' he continued, as though she hadn't spoken, 'Dublin is a great city—'

'That's hardly the point! I can't live here with you, Finn—surely you can see that would be impossible?'

There was a long, rather strange pause. 'I wasn't suggesting that you live here with me, Catherine.'

Oh, if only the floor could have opened up and swallowed her! 'Well, thank God for that,' she said, rather weakly, and hoped that her voice didn't lack conviction. 'Where did you have in mind, then? Is there some home for unmarried mothers on the outskirts of the city?'

He had the grace to wince. 'I have a cottage by the sea. It's in Wicklow, close to Glendalough and a relatively short drive away. Fresh air and village life. It would be perfect for you. And the baby.'

It sounded like an oasis. 'I don't know.'

He heard her indecision and, like a barrister moving in for the kill with his closing argument, fluently outlined his case. 'You live on your own in London— what's the difference? And I can come and see you at weekends.'

Once again, she despaired at the sudden race of her pulse. He meant grudging duty visits, nothing else. She shook her head. 'No.'

'There are other factors, too, Catherine.'

She looked up, wishing that it wasn't such painful pleasure to stare into the eyes of the man who had fathered her child. 'Such as?'

'I have some friends who live there—Patrick and Aisling. I can introduce you to Aisling—she'd love to meet you, I'm sure. They've three children of their own—it would be good to have someone like that around.'

Aisling?

The name rang a bell and Catherine remembered

the morning she had left Finn's flat. A woman called Aisling had been talking on the answer-machine, asking where the hell he had been. She had assumed that it was someone he had stood up because he'd had a better offer.

'Do you know more than one Aisling?' she asked.

'No. Why?'

She shook her head. 'It doesn't matter.'

He carried on trying to sell the delights of Greystones, knowing that if she could see the place for herself she'd be sold. 'And my aunt lives there, too.'

'Your aunt?'

'That's right. She's...well, she's a very special lady.'

Catherine swallowed. She could just imagine what a protective relative would have to say about some conniving woman tricking her darling nephew into fatherhood.

'I don't think so, Finn,' she said uncertainly. 'Wouldn't everyone find the situation a little odd?'

'Well, of course they would. No one's ever heard me mention you before, and suddenly here you are— pregnant with my child!'

'Could do your street-cred a lot of harm?' she hazarded sarcastically.

'It's not my reputation I'm thinking about, Catherine,' he said softly. 'It's yours.' His eyes glittered as the spectre of responsibility reared its head. He did not balk it, but faced it head-on. 'There is, of course, one solution which would guarantee you all the respect a woman in your condition warrants.'

Utterly confused now, she stared at him in perplexity. 'What solution?'

'Marry me.'

There was a long, deafening silence and Catherine's heart clenched in her chest. 'Is this some kind of joke?' she demanded hoarsely.

He shook his head. 'Think about it, Catherine—see what sense it makes. It gives you security, for a start. And not just for you, for the baby.'

Perhaps someone else might have considered that offer in a purely mercenary way, but that someone else was not Catherine, with Catherine's experience of the world.

She had never thought about her own mortality much, but right now it was foremost in her mind. New life automatically made you think of the other end of the spectrum.

What would happen to her if she died suddenly? Who would look after and care for the baby? Not her mother, that was for sure.

But if she married Finn...

She stared at him with clear, bright eyes. 'And what's in it for you?'

'Can't a clever journalist like you work it out?' he answered flippantly, but then his voice sobered. 'As an ex-lover I can be sidelined, but as your husband I would have a say in the baby's life. It legitimises everything.' His eyes met hers with sudden under-standing. 'And didn't you say that you didn't want what you had to endure yourself for your baby? Whatever happens, Catherine, this child will have my name—and one day will inherit my wealth.'

'An old-fashioned marriage of convenience, you mean?'

'Or a very modern one,' he amended quietly.

It was a deliberately ambiguous statement. 'And what's that supposed to mean?'

'It means whatever you want it to mean. We can make the rules up as we go along.'

'And how long is this marriage supposed to last—presumably not for life?'

'Presumably not.'

'And if you want out?'

'Or you do?' he countered coolly.

'Either. If the situation between us is untenable in any way, then—'

'Aren't you jumping the gun a little? Why don't we save the big decisions until after the baby is born?'

He gave the glimmer of a smile, and Catherine felt her stomach turn over. Did he have any idea how that smile could turn a normally sensible woman's head? In spite of everything.

'What do you say, Catherine?'

She thought of going through it all alone, and suddenly felt the first tremblings of fear. For a moment she felt small and helpless and vulnerable—though surely that was natural enough?

While Finn was big and strong and dependable. It didn't matter what his feelings for her were, he would protect her, instinct told her that. And instinct was a very powerful influence where pregnant women were concerned.

She looked at him. He had stated that she didn't really have the luxury of choice, and in a way he was right. For what right-minded and responsible woman in her situation could give any answer other than the one which now came from between her dry lips.

'Very well, Finn. I'll marry you.'

CHAPTER TEN

As WEDDINGS went, it was bizarre. The ceremony had to be quick and it had to be discreet—any sign of a hugely pregnant bride would have the press sniffing around in droves, and Finn didn't want that. Neither did Catherine.

And organising a wedding wasn't as easy as they made out in the films.

'Ireland's out,' he'd said grimly, as he replaced the telephone receiver. 'You need three months' written notice.'

'You didn't know that?' The question came out without her thinking.

'Why would I?' His eyes had sparked icy blue fire. 'I've never got married before.'

And wouldn't be now, she'd reminded herself painfully. Not if he hadn't been in such an invidious situation.

'It'll have to be in England, and I have to be resident for seven days prior to giving notice,' he'd said flatly. 'It's fifteen days minimum after that.'

He'd made it sound as if he was to undergo a protracted kind of operation. Catherine had turned away.

They'd flown back to England, where Finn had booked in to a hotel, and by some unspoken agreement they had not seen one another until the day of the wedding itself—although they'd had a few brief, uncomfortable conversations.

Catherine had spent the three weeks trying to behave as normally as possible—seeing her friends, try-ing to write—even once visiting her mother. And all the while her great big secret had burned so strongly within her that she was astonished no one else no-ticed.

When the day of the wedding finally dawned, her most overwhelming emotion was one of relief—that soon the subterfuge would be over.

Catherine glanced at her watch as she waited for her reluctant husband-to-be. She hadn't bought any-thing new—because that also seemed to go against the mood of the arrangement. Her favourite clingy violet dress made her look voluptuous, and she was grateful for the long jacket which covered most of the evidence.

But when she opened the door to him, her face drawn and tense, Finn felt his heart miss a beat.

'Smile for me, Catherine,' he whispered.

Obediently she curved her lips upwards into a smile, trying not to be enticed by the blue gleam of his eyes.

'You look like a gypsy,' he observed softly, as she pinned two large silver hoops to her ears.

'Is that bad, or good?'

'It's good,' he replied evenly, but he had to force himself to walk away and stare sightlessly out of the window. The trouble was that he still wanted her, and yet there now seemed to be an unbreachable emo-tional gulf which made intimacy out of the question. He glanced down at his watch. 'Almost ready to go?'

Nerves assailed her for the hundredth time that morning. He looked so devastating in his dark suit and snowy shirt that she was having difficulty remem-bering that this was all make-believe. He wasn't a *real* groom any more than she was a *real* bride. 'Finn, it's still not too late to back out, you know.'

'You want to?'

Of course she did. Part of her would have loved to be able to wave a magic wand and wish her old life back. While another part wished that this gorgeous man would sweep her into his arms and kiss all her make-up off and tell her that he couldn't bear *not* to marry her.

But of course he wouldn't. It wasn't that kind of deal. This was, to use her own expression—and it was one which had the power to make her giggle in a slight hysteria which she put down to hormones—a marriage of convenience. Modern or otherwise.

'Are you wishing it was Peter?' he asked suddenly.

'Peter?' To her horror she actually had to pause and think who he was talking about.

He heard the tone of her voice and his mouth thinned. That said a lot about her level of commitment, didn't it? 'Yeah, Peter—the man you went out with for—how long was it, Catherine? Four years?'

'Three.' She heard his disapproval and she couldn't bear that he might think she had just leapt from Peter's bed into his. 'We hadn't seen each other for six months before he ended it,' she said slowly. 'And I accepted that it was over.' She turned wide green eyes up to his. 'There was certainly no motive of getting my own back.'

'I see.' But he felt his body relax a little.

'And besides, what about you?' she challenged. 'Are you sorry that it's not Deirdra you're marrying?'

There was a pause. 'Deirdra's history.'

'That doesn't answer my question, Finn.'

He supposed it didn't. 'It happened a long time

ago.' He shrugged. 'We were both seventeen and discovering sex for the first time. It burnt itself out and then she went to Hollywood. End of story.'

He was describing first love, thought Catherine with a pang. And maybe for him—as for so many people—no one would ever live up to that idealised state. First love. There was nothing like it—even hard-bitten Miranda had said that.

'Oh, I see,' she said slowly.

He looked at her assessingly. 'Back out now, if you want to, Catherine.'

'No, I'm happy to go ahead with it,' she said.

'Well, you don't look it,' he said softly. 'You'll have to work harder than that to convince anyone.'

She fixed a smile to her glossy lips. 'How's that?'

'Perfect,' he answered, feeling an ache in his groin which he knew would not be satisfied by a traditional post-wedding night.

For directly after the ceremony they were taking the first flight back to Ireland. A car would be waiting at the airport and he was driving her to Greystones, to settle her into the house.

And after the weekend he would return to Dublin. Alone.

Finn thought how vulnerable she looked on the plane, shaking her head and refusing his offer of a glass of champagne, her face telling him that she had nothing to celebrate.

He had to keep telling himself not to be sucked in by a pair of green eyes and a rose-pink mouth, tell himself instead that Catherine Walker had a bewitching power which hid her true nature. And that beauty combined with burgeoning life could fool a man into thinking she was something different. And, while she might not have conspired to humiliate him publicly, she had still deliberately kept from him the fact that she was a journalist.

'Won't your mother think it strange that you didn't tell her about the wedding?' he asked, as the car left Dublin and began to eat up the miles leading towards the coast.

'Lots of people go away and get married without telling anyone these days.'

'She won't pry?'

'I'll have to tell her the truth—that I'm pregnant,' she said flatly. 'She'll understand.' Oh, yes—her mother would understand *that* all right.

'And when are you going to inform her that you've acquired a husband?'

Acquired a husband! He made it sound like something from a Victorian novel! 'When I'm…settled.'

'Soon?' he demanded.

She nodded. 'Once I've been at Greystones for a couple of days.' Catherine stole a look at Finn's dark profile. 'Have you told your aunt, or any of your friends?'

He shook his head, easing his foot down on the accelerator. 'They'd only have wanted to join in and make a big fuss of it.'

And, presumably, turn the day into something it wasn't.

But repeating her marriage lines after the registrar had made Catherine feel heartbreakingly wistful, and only the stirring flutter in her stomach had kept her voice steady enough to speak in a voice as devoid of emotion as Finn's.

'What a lovely couple you make!' the Registrar had

cooed, and then said with a twinkle, 'You may now kiss your wife.'

Finn had looked down at Catherine, a wry smile touching the corners of his lips as he saw the startled look which widened her green eyes. 'Mustn't disappoint, must we?' he'd murmured, and bent his head to brush his mouth against hers.

As kisses went, it had been almost chaste. Not deep and hungry and greedy, like the kisses they had shared before they had made love. But, in its way, the most poignant kiss of all—gentle and full of false promise. His lips were like honey and just the touch of them had sent little shivers of longing all the way down her spine. And yet it had mocked her with all that it could have been and was not.

Not for them the urgent and giggling drive to the nearest bed to consummate the marriage. Instead she would be delivered to a house which—although it sounded quite lovely—was to be hers alone during the week, while the baby grew inside her belly.

And after that?

Resisting the urge to wrap her arms around his neck, Catherine had pulled away, giving the watching registrar an awkward smile.

They arrived at Greystones late in the afternoon, through sleepy-looking streets and past stone houses. Finn's cottage stood at the far end of the small town, an unprepossessing low stone building which looked as though it had been there since the beginning of time.

'Oh, it's beautiful, Finn,' she said, breathing in the sea-air and thinking what a healthy place this was to be when she compared it to her tiny flat in London.

And she was healthy, too—the bloom of pregnancy making her face seem to glow from within. She looked both fragile and strong, and on an impulse Finn bent and scooped her up into his arms, his eyes glittering blue fire as he looked down into her face.

'What the h-hell do you think you're doing?' she spluttered.

'Bowing to tradition, as well as bowing my head,' he said softly, as he bent his head to carry her through the low door. 'By carrying you over the threshold.'

He placed her down carefully, seeming reluctant to remove his hands from her waist, and Catherine stared up into his face. 'Why did you do that?'

'It'll soon get round that I've married you. We ought to maintain at least a modicum of pretence that it's the real thing.'

She pulled away. It hurt just as much as it was probably intended to, and Catherine had to remind herself that she had walked into this with her eyes open. She had agreed to marry him for the sake of her baby and her baby alone—but that didn't stop her from having the occasional foolish fantasy, did it? Didn't stop her from wishing that they didn't have to go through a hypocritical stage-managed act just in case anyone happened to be watching them.

In an attempt to distract herself she looked around her instead. The cottage was comfortably furnished with squashy sofas, and paintings of wild and wonderful Wicklow were hung everywhere. But the walls were surprisingly faded—indeed, the whole room looked as though it could do with a coat of paint.

'Come through here,' said Finn, looking at the stiff and defensive set of her shoulders. 'I've something to show you.'

The smaller room which led off the sitting room looked similarly tired, but Catherine's attention was soon drawn from the state of the walls by a desk overlooking the big garden at the back of the house. Because what was on it stood out like a sore thumb. A desk with a high-tech computer, fax and telephone and state-of-the-art printer—all obviously and gleamingly new.

'For you,' he said simply.

Catherine looked longingly at the computer, which made her own look as if it had been invented around the same time as the wheel, then lifted her face up to him. 'Why?'

'A wedding present.'

'I've bought nothing for you—'

He shook his head. 'You write, don't you? I thought that as you were going to be living in a remote place you might as well have the most modern stuff on the market to keep you in touch with the big world outside.'

'I've brought my own computer,' said Catherine stubbornly.

'I imagined you would have done—but I doubt it has anything like the speed or the power of this one.'

She turned on him furiously. 'You don't have to *buy* me, you know, Finn!'

'For God's sake—do you have to be so damned defensive? You wouldn't *be* here if I had been thinking with my head instead—'

'You don't have to spell it out for me,' she said in a hollow voice, feeling quite sick. 'And there's no need for you to play the martyr, either.'

'I am not playing the martyr,' he retorted. 'I am just taking responsibility for your predicament—'

'Stop it! Just stop it!' she interrupted, even angrier now. 'I will not, *not* have this baby described as a "predicament". It wasn't planned, no—but it's happened and I intend to make the best of it. This baby is going to be a *happy* baby, whatever happens. And you shan't take the lion's share of the responsibility, either. We're both to blame, if you like.'

'Blame?' He gave an odd smile. 'Now who's using loaded words, Catherine?' But he forced himself to draw back, to blot out lips which when furiously parted like that made him want to crush them beneath his own. And to try to put out of his mind the fact that to spend the rest of the afternoon in bed might just rid them both of some of their pent-up anger.

And frustration, he thought achingly.

'Would you like to get changed?' he asked, eyeing the purple dress which clung so provocatively to her blossoming body and wondering how he was going to get through the weekend with any degree of sanity.

Catherine nodded. 'Please.'

'Come on, I'll show you upstairs.'

There were four bedrooms, though one was almost too tiny to qualify.

Finn put her suitcase on the bed of the largest room, which suddenly seemed like the smallest to her, when he was close enough to touch and she was beguiled by a faint, evocative trace of his aftershave.

'The bathroom's along the corridor,' he said quickly. 'You'll find everything you need.'

She had a quick bath and then struggled into her jeans, throwing a baggy jumper over the top. When she came downstairs she found that Finn had changed as well.

He saw her frowning. 'What's up?'

'My jeans won't do up!' she exclaimed, pointing at the waistband.

He hid a smile. 'That's generally what happens, Catherine. We'll have to buy you some pregnancy clothes—though God knows where around here!'

'Big tent-like dresses with Peter Pan collars!' she groaned.

'No, not any more,' he said knowledgeably.

Her eyes narrowed. 'How do you know that?'

'I remember Aisling telling me, the last time she was pregnant. Come on and I'll make you tea,' he said. 'And then I'll light a fire.'

She followed him into a kitchen which had most definitely not been modernised, and Catherine raised her eyebrows in surprise at the old-fashioned units and the brown lino on the floor. Even the ugly windows hadn't been replaced!

'How long have you owned this place, Finn?'

He turned the tap on and filled up the kettle, his back to her. 'It came on the market about five years ago.'

She heard the evasion in his voice and wondered what he wasn't telling her. She raised her eyebrows. 'It's not the kind of place I imagined you buying. It's…well, it's nothing like your place in Dublin.'

'No.' He had forgotten for a moment that she was a journalist, with a journalist's instinct for a story. *His* instinct would be not to tell it. But they were married now, even if it was in name only. And if she was going to give birth to his baby then what was the point in keeping everything locked in? 'It's where I was born. Where I lived until the age of seven.'

Catherine studied him. There was something else here, too—something which made his voice deepen with a bleak, remembered pain. She wondered what had happened to him at the age of seven.

He saw the question in her eyes and sighed, knowing that he had to tell her. She carried his baby, and that gave her the right to know about a past he had grown used to locking away. 'My mother died,' he said, in stark explanation, bending down to light the gas with a match.

'I'm sorry—'

'She'd been widowed when I was a baby—there was no one left to look after me and so I went to live with my aunt.'

'Oh, Finn.' Her heart went out to him, and she wanted to put her arms tightly round him and hug away his pain, but the emotional shutters had been banged tightly shut. She could read that in the abrupt way he had turned away, putting cups and saucers upon a tray with an air of finality. Catherine understood the need for defence against probing into pain. The time was not right—indeed, it might never be right. But that was Finn's decision, not hers.

'Have you such a thing as a biscuit?' she asked, with a smile. 'I'm starving!'

He let out a barely perceptible sigh. 'There's enough food to sink a battleship. I asked Aisling to come in and stock up on groceries. We don't have to go out all weekend, if we don't want to.'

Catherine's smile faded and she couldn't quite work out whether she felt excitement or terror. What did that mean? she wondered, with a slight tinge of hysteria. That play-acting as honeymooners was going to extend as far as the bedroom?

'Go and sit down, Catherine,' he commanded softly. 'And I'll bring this through.'

His face was unreadable in the dying light of the day, and rather dazedly Catherine obeyed him, sinking down onto one of the squashy sofas while she struggled not to project too much. There was no point in working out what she would do if he suggested bed when the circumstance might never arise!

He brought the tea in and poured her a cup.

'Is today a sugar day, or not?' he asked gravely.

She bit back a smile, stupidly pleased that he had remembered. 'Not. My cravings seem to have settled down into something approaching a normal appetite.' She waited until she had drunk some of the tea, then put the cup down. 'Finn?'

'Catherine?'

'How often do you come to stay here?'

'Not often enough,' he admitted. 'I keep meaning to spend weekends here, to get a breath of sea-air and a bit of simple living to blow the cobwebs away, but...' His words tailed off.

'But?'

'Oh, you know what it's like. Life seems to get in the way of plans.'

Yes, she knew what it was like—or rather what it *had* been like. But she was beginning a whole new life now, and a whole new future. And not just in terms of the baby. She was going to be living in Finn's cottage as his quasi-wife and she didn't have a clue about what role she was supposed—or wanted—to fulfil! Make up the rules as we go along, he had said, but surely that was easier than he suggested?

But for the baby's sake she cleared her thoughts of concern and settled down to drink her tea.

He saw the softening of her face, and the look of

serenity which made a Madonna of her, and found himself wondering how many different masks she wore. Or was her pregnancy just making him project his own idealised version of her as the future mother of his child? That she was soft and caring and vulnerable…rather than the cynical and go-getting journalist.

Life is evidence-based, Finn, he reminded himself grimly. Just think of the evidence. She wears different masks, that's all. Just as all women do.

He stood up. 'I'll light the fire,' he said shortly.

Catherine felt unreal and disconnected as he created a roaring blaze from the logs in the basket, and warmth and light transformed the room just as dusk crept upon the early evening air. The flames cast shadows which flickered over the long, denim-clad thighs and she remembered their powerful strength in different guises. Running through a Greek sea. Naked and entwined with hers.

He looked up to find her watching him, her slim body sprawled comfortably on the sofa, and the temptation to join her and to kiss her almost overwhelmed him. He knew that in her arms he could forget all his doubts and misgivings about the bizarre situation they had created for themselves.

But wouldn't being intimate with her tonight make a bizarre situation even more so? Confuse and muddy the waters?

He caught her eye but she quickly looked away, as if uncomfortable, and Finn was forced to acknowledge that things had changed, that there was no guarantee that Catherine wanted him in that way any more. Not after everything that had happened.

Later she unpacked, and Finn cooked them supper,

and afterwards they listened to Irish radio until she began to yawn and escaped to her bedroom. Her senses and thoughts were full of him. All she could think about was how much she wanted him.

And how much easier everything would be if she didn't.

But, after a surprisingly sleep-filled night alone on the big, soft feather mattress, the morning dawned bright and sunny. After breakfast Finn took her down to the beach to look at the boats and to walk along the sand, then afterwards to meet his aunt.

Her heart was beating nervously as they approached the house. 'What's her name?'

'Finola.'

'I bet she'll take an instant dislike to me.'

'Don't be silly, Catherine—she's hardly going to hate a woman I bring home and introduce as my wife, now, is she? She loves me; she wants me to be happy.'

Happy? What an ironic choice of word.

'So what's your definition of happiness, Finn?'

He stooped down for a pebble and hurled it out at the blue sea before turning to look at her with eyes which rivalled the ocean's hue.

'It's a way of travelling, Catherine,' he said slowly. 'Not a destination.'

So, was she happy at this precise moment? She thought about it. Actually, yes, she was. Though contented was probably a better description. She was healthy and pregnant and walking along a beautiful beach with a beautiful man. And if she defined happiness in a futile wish that their relationship went deeper than that, then she was heading for a big disappointment. You couldn't look for happiness in another person. First you had to find it within yourself.

She thought that to the outside world they probably made a very striking couple—both tall and slim, with matching heads of jet-black, and her gleaming and brand-new gold band proclaiming very definitely that she was a newly-wed.

But there were several giveaway signs that all was not as it appeared. Finn did not smile down into her face with the conspiratorial air of a lover, nor hold her hand as if he couldn't bear to let it go.

Not, that was, until they arrived at his aunt's house. Then he caught her fingers in his and squeezed them reassuringly. 'It'll be okay,' he whispered.

The door was opened by a grey-haired woman in her late sixties, whose faded eyes were a blue a few shades less intense than those of her nephew. She only came up to the middle of his chest, but she flung her arms around him all the same and Catherine's heart clenched as he hugged her back. She'd never seen him so openly affectionate and demonstrative.

'Why, it's the divil himself!' she exclaimed. 'Finn! Finn Delaney!' She fixed him with a look of admonishment, but anyone could see her heart wasn't in it. 'And why haven't you been round to see me sooner?' Without waiting for an answer, she moved the blue eyes curiously from Finn to Catherine. 'And who might this be?'

Catherine was feeling as nervous as a child on the first day of school, recognising how much this woman meant to Finn and desperately not wanting to start off on the wrong foot.

'I'm Catherine,' she said simply. 'I'm Finn's wife.'

CHAPTER ELEVEN

Finn's wife.

The first and only time she had said it had been to Finn's aunt, but she thought it often enough, running the words sweetly through her mind like chocolate melting over ice-cream.

She had thought it the first morning he had driven back to Dublin, standing in the doorway just like a proper wife, watching his car disappear over the horizon, leaving her alone with her thoughts and her writing and her growing baby. And the big bed in which she slept alone.

The car had become a distant dot and she'd slowly closed the door on it, telling herself that she was glad he had made no move to consummate the marriage.

It would have only complicated things. Made the inevitable split more difficult—for her, certainly. Because women grew much closer to a man when they had sex with him. Even more so when that man's child grew bigger with every day that passed.

But being off limits had forced them together in a way which had its own kind of intimacy. For what did you do when you were closeted together every weekend and unable to do the one thing you most wanted to do?

Well, they seemed to go for an awful lot of walks. Brisk, bracing walks along the unimaginably beautiful coastline. He would feed her cream and scones, and afterwards take her back to the cottage and insist that she put her feet up for the inevitable sleep which would follow. Sometimes she would wake up to find him watching her, the blue eyes so blazing and intent. And for one brief and blissful moment she would almost forget herself, want to hold her arms out towards him, to draw him close against the fullness of her breasts.

But the moment would be lost when he turned away, as if something he saw in her disturbed him, and she wondered if he felt uncomfortable with this masquerade of marriage. Did he find himself wanting to tell the aunt who was more like a mother to him that it was not all it seemed? That he had made her pregnant and was simply doing the right thing by her? Was he now perhaps regretting that decision?

He'd taken her to meet his friends who lived at the far end of the small town. Apparently he had known Patrick 'for ever', and Patrick's wife, Aisling, was an energetic redhead who squealed with delight when they told her the news.

'At last!' she exclaimed. 'You've done it at last! Oh, Finn—there'll be legions of women weeping all over Ireland!'

'And legions of men sighing with relief,' commented Patrick wryly as he reached into the fridge for a bottle of champagne.

'Shut up.' Finn smiled.

'So you went and got married *without telling anyone*?' Patrick demanded as he eased the cork out of the bottle. 'Even us?'

'Especially you,' murmured Finn. 'We didn't want the whole of Wicklow knowing!' He paused. 'Catherine's pregnant, you see.'

'Oh, Patrick,' said Aisling softly. 'Will you listen

to the man? ''Catherine's pregnant,'' he says. As if we didn't have eyes in our heads, Finn Delaney! Congratulations! To both of you!'

She hugged them both in turn and Catherine felt a great lump rise in her throat, glad to have her face enveloped in Aisling's thick-knit sweater. I don't deserve this, she thought. I can't go through with it. Pretending to these nice people that all is what it seems.

But she looked up, her eyes bright, and met a sudden warm understanding in Finn's, and she drew an odd sort of comfort from that.

'Will you look after Catherine for me while I'm away in Dublin, Aisling?' he said, his voice suddenly urgent.

'But I don't need looking after!' protested Catherine, slightly terrified that this attractive woman with the warm smile might ask questions which would be impossible not to answer truthfully.

'You can see me as much or as little as you wish to, Catherine—I won't mind in the least,' said Aisling firmly. 'But won't you be terribly lonesome with Finn away?'

'Catherine wanted peace and quiet,' put in Finn. 'So Dublin's out. And she wants to write.'

'Yes.' Catherine swallowed. 'I'm a journalist.'

'So I believe,' said Aisling lightly, leaving Catherine wondering whether she had read the article. But even if she had she didn't seem to hold it against her, not judging by the genuine warmth of her welcome, anyway.

A small boy came running in, closely followed by an older sister, his face covered in sand and the sticky remains of a crab. 'Jack Casey! Just what have you been doing to yourself?'

'He tried to eat the crab, Mammy!' crowed the little girl. 'Even though I told him not to!'

'And you just let him, did you?' asked her mother, deftly picking up a cloth and beginning to scrub at her protesting son. 'Does this not put you off what you're about to go through, Catherine?'

'Well, I'll have a few years to prepare myself,' said Catherine, as Jack deposited a chubby handful of shells into her lap.

'Jack! Please don't put sand all over Catherine's dress!' scolded Aisling.

'I don't mind—honestly, I don't.'

Finn sat and watched the interaction of everyday family life and felt a great clench of his heart. How easy and uncomplicated it all seemed on the surface. With Catherine sitting there laughing as a sticky hand was shoved towards her hair, which today she had woven into two thick plaits which fell over her breasts.

Pregnancy suited her, he thought unwillingly, and her growing body seemed just as sexy as the pre-pregnancy one had done.

Thank God he was going back to Dublin in the morning!

The weeks slid by and Catherine settled into her new life, taking to the slow, easy pace like a duck to water.

She rose early and walked along the seashore, tracing her route back via the shops, where she bought freshly baked bread and milk which tasted better than any milk she had ever drunk before.

Then she settled down to write, but found that her

writing had changed. She no longer had the desire nor the contacts to produce the punchy, easy-read features which had defined her career up until this point.

The flat in Clerkenwell was being rented out at an exorbitant fee, and so for the first time in her life there were no pressing money worries. She could enjoy her pregnancy and give in to what she most wanted to do.

She began to write a book.

'You're the only person I've told!' she said on the phone to her mother one night.

'What, not even Finn?'

'No. It's a surprise,' said Catherine truthfully. Or was she scared of trying and failing in his eyes?

'And when am I going to meet this husband of yours?' asked her mother. 'Everybody's asking me what he's like and I have to tell them that I don't know!'

This was a difficult one—more than difficult. Catherine had the means to fly her mother out—and knew how much she wanted to see her and how much her mother would enjoy life in the small Irish village. But—and it was a monumental but—how did she begin to explain the situation?

If her mother came she would either have to tell the truth or she would have to pretend, and she didn't know how long she could keep that up in front of the person who knew her so well.

For a start she and Finn would be expected to share a bedroom, and she knew for a fact that she couldn't do it. Couldn't sleep with him and not be climbing the walls with a terrible yearning to have him close to her in a way he did not want to be. It was bad enough on her nights alone, and the ones when he was sleeping just along the corridor—being in an enclosed space with a bed in it would be almost impossible.

'Soon, Mum,' she said lamely.

'If you leave it much longer, then I'll be a grandmother!'

And that might be the best solution all round. Wait until the baby was born and the disruption he or she would cause would detract from what was actually going on in Finn and Catherine's so-called relationship. And besides, no one expected a new mother to be energetically making love to her husband every night!

Having another person in the house would mean that Finn would be able to focus on the best thing to do. And so would she. They could come to an amicable agreement about access, and all the other things people had to discuss when they were no longer together.

Not that she and Finn had ever been together. Not really. Not in the true sense of the word, anyway.

But it was funny how you could grow close to someone, even though your head was telling you that it was sheer madness to do so. She didn't want to find him funny and sexy and engaging. She wanted to be able to pick holes in his character, to tell herself that actually he was a cold and power-hungry maniac and that she would never have been happy with him anyway.

But she couldn't.

She told herself that it was easy to get on well with someone over the course of a weekend—that if they lived together all the time they would irritate the hell out of each other. But she couldn't quite believe that, either.

Energy flowed through her like lifeblood. She wrote throughout the day, sometimes well into the evening, and when Finn rang she would tell him how her day had been. They would talk with an ease and familiarity which was poignant in itself.

One night she told him how she'd been over and helped Aisling with her baking, and that Aunt Finola had taken her to a bingo session at the church hall and Catherine had won an ironing board!

'What are you going to do with it?'

'I gave it to the priest's housekeeper. It seems silly to have two.'

'Could come in useful,' he said gravely.

'As an extra table, perhaps?' she suggested helpfully.

She told herself that of course it was easy to talk to someone on the phone, because you couldn't see the expression on their face or the look in their eyes. She told herself that it was important they remained on good terms because she would need to be in touch with Finn for the rest of her life. The baby would always connect them.

And she told herself that she would be okay when the day came—perhaps sooner than she would hope for—when he would tell her gently that the time had come for the parting of the ways. That they had done their best for the baby and now they were both free.

But she didn't want to be free. Or was that simply sneaky Mother Nature again—tying her emotionally to the biological father of her child?

It didn't seem to matter how much logic warned her that she mustn't embrace her new-wife role too enthusiastically, because try as she might she couldn't help herself.

Every Friday night she felt like a woman whose husband was coming home like a conquering hero. She would see the city-strain etched on his face as he opened the front door and she would pour him a gin and tonic—just like a real wife.

Finn found he couldn't wait to be out of the city on Friday nights, tying up his work as early as possible so that he could be roaring out of Dublin and heading for the sea.

His apartment now seemed very empty in a way that the cottage never did. But Catherine did girly things; maybe that was why. She put flowers in vases and she baked cakes. Any day now he was fully expecting her to have acquired a new puppy!

She's just playing another role—a domestic role this time, he told himself, as the glitter of the distant sea told him he was almost home. But surely she wouldn't be able to keep it up for ever?

He walked into the cottage one night and frowned. Something was different, and it took a moment or two to figure out what it was.

'You've painted the walls!'

'So I have.' She gave a serene smile as she walked over to the drinks tray, pleased with the soft-peach wash which had transformed the dingy room. 'Do you like it?'

He looked around, his expression closed yet edgy, trying to distract himself from the pink V-necked sweater she wore, which showed far too much of the heavy swell of her breasts and seemed far too provocative for a cold Friday night in Wicklow!

'You should have asked me first!' he ground out.

The smile died on her lips. 'I'm sorry, Finn,' she said stiffly. 'I was mistakenly using the place as my home, perhaps fooling myself a little too convincingly that we were a married couple!'

'Even if we were,' he came back bitingly, 'surely decorating is something a couple would discuss together?'

'I wanted to surprise you—'

'Well, you've certainly done that, Catherine!'

And then he turned on her, his blue eyes blazing with an anger which was surely disproportionate to the crime of painting a room.

'Don't you think that if I'd wanted it decorated I'd have done so before, myself? Don't you think I'd have had the best decorators in the damned country working for me?'

She slammed his gin and tonic down so hard that it slopped all over the sideboard, but she was too angry to care and Finn didn't seem to notice.

'Oh, I'm *sorry*! The best money can buy? Is that what you mean?' she questioned witheringly. 'Is that why you're so mad? Because I was stupid enough to do it myself? Because I picked up the paintbrush instead of snapping my fingers to get someone else to do it for me? Well, don't you worry, Finn Delaney— I happened to be very careful. And if I say so myself I did a *bloody good job*—even if you're too stupid and too arrogant to see it!'

And she stormed out of the room and up the stairs.

'Catherine, just you come right back here!'

'Go to hell! Except they'd probably turn you away!' she yelled back.

He took the stairs two at a time and reached her just as she was about to close the bathroom door, puffing and out of breath. She saw him coming and tried to slam it, but he stuck his foot in it.

'Get your foot out!'

'Not until you open it!'

'I want a bath!'

'And I want to talk to you!'

'Well, tough! If you want to complain about the wretched walls again, then don't worry—we'll go out in the morning and get some peat and rub it in. Then they'll look as dingy as before.'

He started to laugh, and she took the opportunity to push at the door again.

'Open the door, Catherine.'

'Open it yourself!' But she let go and he stepped inside, dwarfing the room with his powerful presence.

He saw the defiant yet defeated droop of her shoulders and something inside him melted. 'Oh, sweetheart, I'm sorry. I shouldn't have spoken to you like that!'

'You should have thought before you opened your stupid mouth! But you never do!'

'Yes, I should. And, no, I don't.' He gave a rueful smile. 'But I think we've already established that my thinking goes out of the window whenever you're around, Catherine!'

'Then maybe we should reconsider this whole stupid scheme!'

'You think it's stupid?'

'I think that we must be out of our minds to think we can go through with it, yes!'

'But I thought you were enjoying life down here—'

'Oh, you *stupid* man!'

He burst out laughing. 'You know, for a journalist, you're having terrible trouble with your command of the English language, Catherine. That's three times you've used the word ''stupid'' in as many—'

Her hand flew up to slap his face, but he caught it, using it to pull her right up close to him, and she saw that he was having difficulty controlling his breathing, that his blue eyes had suddenly darkened like the night.

'My, my, my, but you've a temper on you like a witch sometimes!'

'And is it any wonder, living with you?'

They stared at one another and the air was suddenly tight with tension.

'Do you know we're arguing like an old married couple?' he said unsteadily. 'You realise that we're getting all the worst bits out of marriage with none of the best bits?'

Something in his eyes was making her feel very dizzy. 'Finn?' she whispered.

'Catherine?' he answered unsteadily.

She knew that he was about to kiss her even before he moved. She could read it in the blue blaze of his eyes. And she opened her lips to greet his, not caring about the wisdom of it, only knowing that she had prayed for this moment ever since he had slipped that gold wedding band on her finger.

They kissed as if it was the first time, and in a way maybe it *was* the first time. This time they were not strangers, drawn together by a hunger which could not be denied. The hunger clamoured as ever before, but now they had a history—past and present and future all fusing together—made flesh by the baby which kicked in her belly.

He drew his mouth away and looked down into her

hectic green eyes, shaken by the power of that kiss. 'God, Catherine,' he said unsteadily.

Rocked by emotions she scarcely recognised, she shook her head. 'Just shut up and kiss me again.'

'Impatient woman,' he said, almost tenderly.

'Impatient?' she demanded incredulously.

'Shut up, Catherine.'

And their lips met again.

He ran his hand down over the fullness of her breast, alighting with possessive greed on the tight curve of her belly, and groaned against her lips as he felt the seeking urgency of her own.

'Catherine—sweet, beautiful, swollen Catherine—let me make love to you now.'

'Swollen' should not have sounded so erotic to her ears, but it did. More than erotic. But she was so aroused at that moment that if he had started reciting the telephone directory to her then it would have sounded like poetry.

She tore her mouth away with difficulty. 'Sweet heavens, Finn—I thought you'd never ask!'

Shakily, his hand traced the outline of her face. He cupped it between his hands and dropped soft kisses onto the pale silk of her skin. He wanted long, slow lovemaking, and he knew that he must be gentle with her, but—dear heaven—he felt so hard, so exquisitely hard, that if she had not been pregnant with his child then he might very well have pushed her to the floor and...

That particular memory drew him up with a jolt, and he allowed himself one fleeting and bitter regret that their child had not been conceived in love but in anger. But that did not matter now. What was done was done, and he now had the opportunity to make the kind of long, slow love which a woman like Catherine deserved.

'Come with me, sweetheart.'

'Where are you taking me?'

'Somewhere I should have taken you weeks ago.' It was a bed he wanted, and the nearest would do— which just happened to be Catherine's room. He spotted a filmy little thong protruding from the top drawer and gave a little shudder as he drew her into the circle of his arms. Could she still wear skimpy underwear like that, even though she was pregnant? He guessed that he was about to find out.

Still holding her with his hands, he pushed her away. 'I've never undressed a pregnant woman before,' he murmured.

'I should hope not!'

'I'll be very careful,' he promised, as he peeled her sweater over her head.

She looped her arms around his neck and followed with the nuzzle of her lips. 'Not too careful, I hope. And besides, it doesn't matter now!'

He smiled. 'That wasn't what I was talking about, and you know it. I meant because you're pregnant.'

'Pregnant women are very resilient—or hadn't you noticed?'

Oh, yes—he'd noticed all right. She wasn't one of those women who lay around like an invalid, expecting to be waited on. Why, just the other day he had had to forcibly remove a spade from her hand and tell her that it was too cold to be digging. She had become huffy and stomped off, and told him that it was a crime not to foster love on such a beautiful garden.

He sucked in a breath as her body was revealed to him. Her breasts were glorious, ripe and bursting as they pushed against ivory-coloured lace. And the matching lacy thong left very little to the imagination.

'God,' he moaned. 'I'd no idea that a pregnant woman could look so sexy!'

'Well, that's a relief,' she offered drily.

He unclipped her bra and the heavy breasts came spilling out. He bent his head and his tongue licked luxuriantly against one hard, dark nipple. Catherine clutched at him, dizzy with the sheer sensation of it.

'Finn,' she said weakly.

'Mmm?'

He tugged at the little lacy thong, sliding it down over her thighs, and laid his hand softly on the dark fuzz of hair which concealed the very core of her femininity. He felt her jerk with pleasure. Wanted to give her yet more pleasure.

He knelt in front of her as if in homage, then dipped his tongue to delve into her honeyed warmth. She clutched his head to her, catching sight of their reflected image in the mirror. The sight of it turned her on even more. It seemed outrageously provocative to see her naked, pregnant body and the dark-haired man working such magic with his mouth.

'I'd better get horizontal,' she groaned. 'Before I fall over.'

He lifted his head and saw the smoky look in her eyes. 'Yeah. I think you'd better.'

He carried her, protesting, but only half-heartedly.

'Finn, stop it—I'm much too heavy these days.'

'But I like it. I like carrying you.'

'I'd noticed!'

'And you're still light enough not to trouble me.'

'You're a very strong man, Finn Delaney,' she sighed.

'I know I am,' he teased.

But he felt as weak as a pussycat as he tore his clothes off and lost himself in the warmth of her embrace.

He kissed her long and hard, smoothing his hand reverentially over her belly, and was just about to move it along, down to the inviting softness of her thighs, when she shook her head.

'Wait,' she whispered.

'I don't think I *can*—'

'Your baby, Finn. He's going to kick.'

'How can you tell?'

'I just can—ouch!'

Finn felt the hefty swipe of a small heel as it connected with the flat of his hand, and he stared down into Catherine's eyes, more shaken than he would have imagined.

'You think it's a boy?' he questioned thickly.

'I think so.'

'How?'

'I don't know…I just… Oh, *Finn*!'

'Do you like that?'

He wasn't feeling the baby any more. 'Mmm.' She slipped her hand down luxuriously, to capture the silken-steel of him, exultant to feel him shudder helplessly beneath her caress. 'Do *you* like that?'

'It's not me I'm thinking of right now—I don't want to hurt you, Catherine.'

For a moment she closed her eyes. If only he knew that the only way he was going to hurt her was by leaving her. And this is only going to make it harder, whispered the voice of reason. You should stop it right now.

But how could she possibly stop him when she wanted him so badly?

'What shall we do?' he whispered.

For a moment she thought he was asking about their future—but his fingers were playing with her breasts, sending little shivers of exquisite sensation rippling like warm sun across her skin. 'You mean *how* shall we…?'

'Mmm.'

'Use your imagination, Finn—I'm as much of a novice at this kind of thing as you are. I—oh, *Finn*!' She gave an expectant wriggle as Finn turned her onto her side and began to stroke her bottom, the other hand sliding up around her waist and from there to cup a swollen breast. She felt him pressing against her, so hard and so ready.

He felt her heat, sensed her urgency. He would never normally have asked a woman if she was ready, but he needed to be sure. And not just because she was pregnant.

'Catherine?' he questioned unsteadily.

'Oh, yes, Finn. Yes!'

Her senses seemed more highly tuned than they had ever been, and she was not sure whether that was down to abstinence or pregnancy. But as he entered her Catherine's mind cleared and she identified the emotion she had not before dared analyse.

For it was love, pure and simple. She loved this man. This man who could never truly be hers. She closed her eyes tightly. Stopped thinking and started feeling. Less pain that way.

Afterwards they lay exactly as they were, like sweat-sheened spoons, their heartbeats gradually slowing along with their breathing.

SHARON KENDRICK 163

He looped a careless arm around her belly and felt another kick. He smiled against her shoulder. 'Ouch, again!'

'You should feel it from inside!'

He levered himself up onto one elbow to stare down at her, brushing back a strand of black hair, his eyes serious. 'I'm sorry I snapped at you.'

'You were frustrated, I expect. Don't worry about it, Finn—so was I.'

His face darkened. 'You think that's what it was all about? Frustration?'

'I don't know, do I? I'm trying to be practical.' Trying not to read too much into this situation and having to fight very hard with herself not to. 'What was it about, if not frustration?'

He turned onto his back, noticing for the first time the old-fashioned embossed wallpaper which covered the ceiling. Would she have ripped *that* down, the next time he came home—and would it really matter if she did? 'You just happened to touch a raw nerve.'

'Because I went ahead and decorated without asking you? Because I took control away from you?'

Would it sound crazy to tell her? Was it crazier still to have her think that he was the kind of intolerant tyrant who insisted on being privy to every decision made inside the home?

He shook his head, wondering if she had become a journalist because she was perceptive, or whether perception had come as a by-product of her career. Or was this just what happened naturally when a man and a woman started living together—started to know one another inside and out? Surely it weakened your defences to let someone get inside your head? Strengthened the relationship, yes, but at what cost?

'What, Finn?' she persisted softly.

'More a case of burying my head in the sand, I guess. Arrested development—call it what you like. A crazy urge to hang on to the past—I'm not sure, Catherine.'

She rested her head on his shoulder. 'You're talking in riddles.'

He smoothed her hair absently. 'I never changed this house at all, you see. I wanted to have it exactly the way it was.'

She thought about this for a moment. 'Like Miss Havisham in *Great Expectations*, you mean?'

'Well, I haven't got a wedding dress covered in cobwebs, if that's what you're implying!' He wound a strand of hair around his finger. 'I suppose this place always represented where I came from. I felt it would be a kind of betrayal if I decorated the interior so that it looked like something you'd find in a magazine.'

'If you applied that theory to everything then we'd still be travelling by horse and cart,' she said reasonably.

He laughed. 'Perhaps.'

She looked at his pensive profile. Was it only in bed that a man like this let his guard down? 'You don't need material things to remind you of your roots, Finn,' she told him softly. 'The values you learned are what matters, and you keep those deep in your heart.'

He nodded. This felt close. Dangerously close. A warm haven far away from the rest of the world. He forced himself to return to reality—because reality was the one thing he was equipped to deal with. He turned to face her and ran a lazy finger down her side, enjoying her responsive shiver. 'So I guess this means we'll be sharing a bedroom from now on?'

It felt like one step forward and two steps back, and all her zing and fizz and exhilaration evaporated. The brightness dimmed and Catherine felt curiously and ridiculously disappointed at his matter-of-fact assessment. Until she reminded herself that nothing had changed—not really.

Their situation was no different from what it had been before, except that now sex had been introduced into the equation. She shouldn't start confusing post-coital confidences with real, true and lasting intimacy.

'I guess we will,' she said lightly. 'Now, are you going to go down and make me my supper? I have a ferocious appetite on me!'

'Ferocious, hmm?' He smiled as he swung his naked body out of bed and looked down at her. 'You know, Catherine, you're sounding more Irish by the day.'

She nodded. She needed to. Her baby was going to be born in Ireland and have an Irish father.

She, too, needed roots.

CHAPTER TWELVE

'CATHERINE! For God's sake, come in here and sit down.'

'I can't! I'm sorting out the kitchen cupboards!'

Finn levered himself up from the sofa and came and stood in the doorway, watching while she bent to work, wondering how a woman eight months into her pregnancy could possibly have such a delectable bottom. He walked over to where she crouched and cupped her buttocks.

'Finn, stop it—'

He bent his head to nuzzle her ear. 'Don't you like it?'

'That's not the point—'

'No?' He kissed the back of her neck. 'The point being what, precisely?'

'I told you—I'm trying to get everything sorted out for when the baby comes.'

'But the baby isn't due for another month,' he objected. 'And I'm flying to London tomorrow. Leave it, Catherine. You won't see me all week.'

'I don't see you all week as it is.' She straightened up with difficulty and allowed him to help her to her feet. 'So what's the difference?'

'A whole sea dividing us?' he teased. 'Won't you miss me?'

She wound her arms around his neck. 'A bit.'

He touched his lips to hers. 'Only a bit?'

Much, much more. 'Stop fishing for compliments!'

'Then come and sit down and have a drink and watch some television.'

She sank onto the sofa. 'What an exciting life we lead, Mr Delaney!'

'Are you complaining?' he asked seriously, as he handed her a glass of sparkling water.

'No, I love it,' she said simply. Just as she loved him. How cosy it all was on the outside. She took a sip and looked at him over the rim of the glass. She had been fidgety over the past few days. Perhaps it was because he was travelling to England. It *was* different, him being in London. A whole plane-ride away. Maybe now was the time to stop pretending that the future was never going to happen.

'Finn?'

'Mmm?'

'There are so many things we haven't discussed.'

'Such as?'

'Well, what happens when the baby's born. What we're going to do—'

'I thought we were taking it a day at a time?'

'And we are.' She drew a deep breath. 'But we can't go on like that for ever, can we?'

He put his glass down. 'I think we could.'

Her heart started beating frantically. 'You do?'

'I can't see any reason why not.' He smiled. 'My sweet Catherine! We've discovered that we like one another. That we can live together without wanting to throw things.' His eyes glittered. 'Thankfully, you seem to have got all that out of your system!' He smiled again as she giggled. 'See! We make each other laugh. We're compatible sexually—though that was never in any question, was it? That's not bad to be going along with.'

'And you think that's enough?'

He got up and threw a log on the fire, because the May weather had taken a sudden, unseasonable dip. It fizzed like a golden firework in the grate and he turned to look down at her, his face all light and shadows cast by the flicker of the flames.

'It's more than a lot of people have,' he said quietly. 'But you must decide whether it's enough for you. Whether you want to go chasing rainbows, or settle for giving this baby the security it deserves. Think about it, Catherine.'

Chasing rainbows. He made the search for love sound so insubstantial. And of course love had been the glaring omission from his list.

'And fidelity?' she asked, because that was more tangible than love.

'I could not tolerate infidelity,' he said slowly. 'And I would not expect you to either.'

Which was not quite the same as saying that the situation would never arise, was it? That if someone came along and captured Finn's heart he wouldn't be off?

'It's up to you, Catherine,' he said. 'The choice is yours. I'm being honest in what I'm offering you.'

Choice. There it was again, that infernal word he was so fond of using and which she was so wary of. Because choice meant coming to a decision, and there was always the chance that she would make the wrong one.

She could give her baby security—and not just the security of being legitimate and being cared for. The security of having a father around. A father who, she was certain, would love the baby as much as she did, who would be the kind of role-model that any small boy would give his eye-teeth for.

He was not offering her rose-tinted dreams and an impossibly romantic future together, but surely that was just practical. And honest, as he had said.

She considered the alternative. Going back out there as a single mother and consigning herself to a life alone with her baby. Or foolishly hoping that she might meet another man who would capture her heart as Finn had done—knowing, deep down, that no other man would ever come close to holding a candle to him.

If they had been different people, with different upbringings and in different circumstances, then both of them might have gone chasing those elusive rainbows.

But they were not different people. They were Finn and Catherine. And their pasts had made them into the people they were today. The past was powerful, she recognised—it sent far-reaching repercussions down through the ages.

'I'll think about it,' she said.

Their lovemaking seemed especially close that night, and they held each other very tightly afterwards for what seemed like a long time.

When Catherine went to the door to wave Finn off in the morning, her heart felt as heavy as the sky.

Finn glanced up at the leaden grey clouds and frowned. 'Feels like snow.'

'You can't have snow in May,' she protested.

'Who says we can't? One year we had a frosting in June!'

'You're kidding?'

'No, sweetheart, I'm not.' He caught her in his arms. 'You will take care, won't you?'

'Of course I will! What do you think I'm going to do? Start snow-boarding? Cross-country skiing?'

'I'm serious.'

She rose up on tiptoe to touch her lips to his. 'And so am I,' she whispered. 'I'll be fine. Ring me when you get to London.'

'Get Aunt Finola to move in if the weather turns bad or if you're worried. Or go and stay with Aisling and Patrick. When are you seeing the doctor next?'

'The day after tomorrow. Finn, stop fussing, will you? Just go!'

His mouth lingered on hers until he drew away reluctantly. 'Better go. Plane to catch.' He held her one last time. 'I'll see you Friday.'

Love you, she thought silently as his car roared away, and she shivered and shut the door.

He rang her from the airport. 'What's the weather like?'

She glanced out at the sky. 'Same.'

'I'll ring you just as soon as I get there.'

'Finn, what's wrong with you? Why are you so worried?'

'What's *wrong* with me? My wife's pregnant and I'm leaving the country! Why on earth should I be worried, Catherine?' he questioned wryly. But he *was* worried. Uneasy. Did every father-to-be feel like a cat on a hot tin roof at a time like this?

Catherine put the phone down and made herself some tea. She glanced at her watch to see that Finn's flight would now be airborne. Keep him safe for me, she prayed, while outside the sky grew darker and the first snowflakes began to flutter down.

It snowed all afternoon, becoming whiter and thicker, until the garden looked just like a Christmas card. Catherine had just lit a fire when there was a loud banging on the door, and there stood Aunt Finola, scarcely recognisable beneath hood and scarf, a rain-mac worn over a thick overcoat and countless sweaters!

'Come in.' Catherine smiled. 'What are you doing out on an afternoon like this?'

'Finn rang me,' explained Finola, shaking snow off her boots. 'Told me to drop in and keep my eye on you.'

'He keeps fussing and fussing!'

'He's worried about you. And the baby.'

'I'm fine.'

'Yes.' Aunt Finola sat down and held her hands out to the heat before sending Catherine a shrewd look. 'You're looking much better these days. Less peaky. More...at peace with yourself,' she finished.

It was an ironic choice of word. 'Well, I'm pleased that's the way I look,' said Catherine slowly.

'You mean it's not the way you feel inside?'

She hesitated. This was Finn's aunt, after all—and in some ways his mother, too. 'I'm fine,' she repeated carefully. 'Honestly.'

'Things seem better between you these days,' observed Aunt Finola carefully. 'You seem more relaxed these past few weeks. The two of yous seemed terrible tense a lot of the time before that.'

Catherine did some sums in her head, and blushed. Oh, God—was it that obvious? That the moment they had starting having sex their relationship had settled down?

'You really love my boy, don't you?' asked Aunt Finola suddenly.

Catherine met her eyes in surprise. But what was the point in lying to someone who loved him, too? Wouldn't she then be guilty of false pride? 'Yes, I love him. Really love him.'

'So why the long face?'

Catherine shook her head. 'I can't talk about it.'

'Well, maybe you can't—but I can. I don't know what went on before Finn brought you here, and I don't want to know, but I assume that he married you because you were pregnant.'

Catherine went very pink. 'Yes,' she whispered. 'Are you shocked?'

Aunt Finola gave a cross between a laugh and a snort. 'Shocked? I'd be a very strange woman indeed to have reached my age and be shocked by something like that! It's been going on since the beginning of time! But Finn's a good man. He'll care for you, stand by you.'

'Yes, but...' Catherine's words tailed away.

'You want more than that, is that it?' Finola nodded her head. 'Tell me, Catherine—is the relationship good, generally?'

'Very good,' Catherine realised, unconsciously beginning to list all the things he had said to her on the eve of his departure. 'We get on, we make each other laugh...' Her cheeks went pink again. 'Oh, lots of things, really. But—'

'But?'

It sounded so stupid to say it. 'He doesn't love me!'

Finola digested this for a moment or two in silence. 'Doesn't he? Are you sure?'

'He never says he does!'

Finola shook her head. 'Oh, you young women to-day!' she said exasperatedly. 'Fed a diet of unrealistic expectations by magazines and books! How many smooth-tongued chancers have you met for whom words are cheap—who tell you they love you one minute and are busy looking over your shoulder at another woman the next? It's not what you say that matters, Catherine, it's what you *do* that counts.'

'You mean you think that Finn loves me?'

'I've no idea what Finn thinks—he never lets me in. He's let no one in, not really—not since he lost his mother.' Her brow criss-crossed in lines of sadness. 'Think about it, Catherine. They'd been everything to each other and suddenly she was taken away, without warning. What child wouldn't have grown wary of love after something like that? Or of expressing it?'

Why had she never looked at it that way before? Her thoughts came tumbling out as words. 'You think I'm being selfish?'

Finola shook her head. 'I think you're not counting your blessings and thinking of all the good things you *do* have. Love doesn't always happen in a blinding flash, Catherine. Sometimes it grows slowly—like a great big oak tree from out of a tiny acorn. And marriages based on that kind of love are sometimes the best in the world. Solid and grounded.' She caught the look on Catherine's face. 'Which doesn't mean to say that they're without passion.'

No. It didn't.

'It all boils down to whether you want instant gratification or whether you are prepared to work for something,' finished Finola gently. 'It's not the modern way, I know.'

'An old-fashioned marriage?' questioned Catherine wryly.

'There was a lot less divorce in those days.' Aunt Finola shrugged. 'People stuck by each other through the good times and the bad times. For richer for poorer. In sickness and in health. Forsaking all others.'

'We got married in a register office,' commented Catherine absently.

'I know you did. But you still made vows, didn't you? Even if you didn't mean them at the time, that doesn't mean they can't be true in the future.'

Catherine nodded. 'Thank you.'

'For?'

'For talking sense to me. For making me realise what's important. I think I really needed to hear it!' She smiled. 'Shall I go and put the kettle on?'

'Now you're talking!'

By morning the world was silent and white, but at least the snow had stopped. Catherine got up as soon as it was light, peering out of the window at the frozen scene with pleasure—until she realised that the path to the gate was completely impassable. Someone could break their leg on that, she thought, especially if it became icy. And so, after a flurry of solicitous phone calls from Finn, Finola and Aisling, Catherine decided to clear the snow away.

She wrapped up warmly and set to work, and several people stopped to talk to her as she cleared the path—most of them asking when the baby was due.

'Not until June,' she told them.

'You've a bit of a wait, then!' said the postman's wife, who had six herself. 'The last month or so's always the worst!'

No one seemed to think it odd that a pregnant woman should be working physically, but that was because, Catherine realised, it wasn't. Not at all. And especially not in rural areas. For centuries women had been working in the fields until they had their babies, and what she was doing wasn't so very different. That morning she felt strong, capable and really *alive*—as if she could conquer the world.

The path was almost cleared when the first pain came, so sharp and so unexpected that Catherine dropped her shovel and held her hands to her tight belly, her breath coming in clouds on the frozen air.

It couldn't possibly be the baby, she reassured herself as the tight spasm receded. The baby wasn't due yet. These pains were nature's way of warning you what the real thing was like.

But the spasms continued throughout the night, and by three o'clock in the morning Catherine could stand it no longer and rang Finola.

'I think it's the baby!' she gasped. 'I think it's coming!'

'Jesus, Mary and Joseph! Don't do a thing. I'm on my way!'

'I couldn't do anything,' said Catherine weakly, and clutched at her middle. 'Even if I wanted to.'

Finola arrived and took one look at her. 'Let's get you straight up those stairs,' she said, 'and then I'm calling the doctor!'

'But I'm supposed to be having the baby in hospital!'

Aunt Finola snorted. 'And how do you suppose we're going to get you to hospital? On a sledge?'

Catherine giggled, and then groaned. 'Don't!' Her

mouth fell open. 'And Finn's supposed to be here! I want Finn here with me.'

'Finn's in London,' said Finola gently. 'Just think about him. Pretend he's here. He'll get here eventually.'

And so he did, by which time Catherine was propped up on the pillows, illuminated by the sunshine which was fast melting the snow, cradling a black-haired baby who was not as tiny as she should have been.

He burst in through the bedroom door, his face a stricken mixture of panic and joy, and was beside the bed in seconds, kissing her nose, her lips, her forehead.

'Catherine! Oh, sweetheart. Sweetheart! Thank God!'

Both Finola and Catherine heard the break in his voice and for one brief moment their eyes met across the room. The expression in the older woman's said as much as, Are you completely *mad*? and Catherine knew that she mustn't wish for the stars. Stars were all very well, but they were a million miles away. This was here. And now. Grounded and safe. Far more accessible than stars.

'You're okay?' he was questioning urgently.

'More than okay,' she said, with the first stirrings of a new-found serenity she suspected came hand in hand with motherhood.

'And is this my daughter?' he was saying in wonder as he stared down at the ebony-dark head and then slowly raised his head to look at his wife. 'My beautiful daughter.'

The soft blue blaze dazzled her, enveloped her in its warmth and wonder. 'Meet Mollie,' she said, and handed him the bundle who immediately began to squeak. 'Miss Mollie Delaney. She hasn't got a middle name yet—we hadn't agreed on one and I thought you might like to—'

'Mary,' he said firmly, as she had known he would. His mother's name.

Finn looked down at the baby in his arms.

'Hello, Mollie,' he said thoughtfully, and when he looked up again his eyes were suspiciously bright.

Aunt Finola made a great show of blowing her nose noisily.

He had come full circle, Catherine realised. Mollie had given him back something of himself. His own childhood had been snatched away from him by the death of his mother and now having his own baby gave him a little of that childhood back.

'What can I say, Catherine?' he said softly. 'Other than thank you.'

At which point his aunt got abruptly to her feet and glared at him. 'I'm off!' she said briskly. 'I'll be back tomorrow!'

After she had gone, the two of them just gazed at their sleeping infant for long, peaceful seconds.

He put the baby down gently in the crib and then sat on the edge of the bed, taking Catherine into his arms as though she was a fragile piece of porcelain which might shatter if he held her too hard.

'Catherine,' he said shakily.

She wanted him closer than this. 'I won't break, you know.'

He pulled her against him and kissed her then, soothed and excited her with just the expert caress of his lips. Catherine sighed with pleasure and then with slight irritation when he stopped, and opened her eyes to find him looking at her rather sternly.

'This changes everything, you know.'

'I know it does. No more sleep, for a start!'

But he shook his head. 'You know what I'm talking about, Catherine.'

That was just the problem. She didn't. Or rather, she didn't dare think about it. Hence her attempt at a joke.

His eyes were burning into her with such intensity—so blue, so beguiling. 'This baby cements what we have between us. You know that, don't you?'

It wasn't the most romantic way he could have put it, but then, whoever said anything about romance? She and Finn were about compatibility and maturity and making the best of a situation they had not chosen. And making the best of things was surely a sound bedrock from which to work?

She recognised, too, that Finn would do all in his power to make sure their relationship flourished—for the sake of Mollie if for nothing else.

She nodded, her eyelids dropping to hide her eyes, afraid that he might see traces of wistful longing there.

'Catherine,' he commanded. 'Look at me.'

She lifted her head and met the soft blue stare.

'Living with you is so easy,' he murmured. 'In so many ways.' There was a pause. 'You make me happy,' he added simply, and he lifted her fingertips to his lips and kissed them.

And if Catherine's heart ached to hear more then she was just being greedy. She made him happy—he had said so. And he made *her* happy. Which was more than most people had. Expecting those three little words said more about society's conventions and expectations than anything else. For how many people said 'I love you' and then proceeded to act as if they didn't? Why, Peter had said it, and then he had run off with someone else!

No, she would count her blessings—and they were legion.

They made each other happy.

Who could ask for anything more than that?

EPILOGUE

CATHERINE sighed a contented sigh. 'Not exactly a conventional honeymoon, is it?'

Finn glanced up from sleepy eyes. In the distance, the dark blue waters lapped rhythmically onto the sand. 'Well, it was never a conventional relationship, was it, sweetheart?' he asked sleepily.

'Finn Delaney, will you wake up and talk to me properly?'

He rolled over onto his back, screwing his eyes up against the bright sunshine, and gave a lazy smile. 'It's all your fault, Mrs Delaney—if you didn't make such outrageous demands on me every minute of every day, then I might be able to keep my eyes open!'

Catherine rubbed a bit more sun-cream onto her tanned arm. 'And you honestly think that Mollie will be okay?'

He propped himself up on one elbow. 'With your mother and Finola looking after her? And Aisling having to be forcibly restrained from dragging her off to the beach every second? Are you kidding, sweetheart? Sounds like bliss for a two-year-old, to me!'

'Mmm. I guess you're right.'

'And anyway—' he pulled her into his arms, feeling the stickiness of the lotion on her skin and pushing his hips against hers in a decidedly provocative way '—I thought we'd decided to do things more conventionally from now on?'

She kissed his neck. 'Mmm.' The church wedding had been conventional enough—even though she had balked at wearing full white bridal regalia. But the snazzy silk suit in softest ivory, purchased from a shop in Grafton Street, had certainly won Finn's approval! And so had the miniature duplicate she had secretly ordered for Mollie!

They had flown out to Pondiki that same afternoon, to discover that Nico had himself found a bride, and was soon to be a father!

Finn gazed at her. 'Are you happy, Catherine?'

'It's a way of travelling, Finn,' she reminded him. 'Not a—Finn!' For he had pulled her onto her back and was lying above her, his gorgeous face only an inch away.

'Are you?' he whispered, his breath warm against her face.

'Blissfully.'

And she was.

Finn now worked from home two days a week—though he claimed that she and his daughter distracted him far too much.

'So what?' she had asked him airily. 'You've enough in the bank, and a bit more besides!'

'Have you a shameless disregard for your future, woman?' he had demanded sternly.

Catherine's mother was a frequent visitor, and she and Finola had struck up a firm friendship.

'Would you ever listen to those two?' Finn would often say, when the rise of their laughter made Mollie giggle. 'What the hell do you think they're concocting now?'

And Mollie continued to thrive. The most beautiful child on the entire planet, as her adoring parents were so fond of saying when they looked at her sleeping every night.

Her early birth, while unexpected, had soon been explained by Catherine's gynaecologist. It seemed that Catherine really *had* got her dates wrong, and that Mollie had been conceived in Dublin, not London, which made her heart lift with pleasure.

'You know what that means, don't you, Finn?' she had asked him.

He certainly did. It meant that their child *had* been conceived in passion, not anger—thank God.

Catherine had abandoned the book she had been writing; she found motherhood much more rewarding. 'Doesn't mean that I'll never write again,' she'd told Finn. 'Just not now.'

And Finn had taken to helping her in the garden sometimes—a plot which she had so transformed that word had spread of its beauty through Wicklow and beyond. Last year she had opened it up to the public, charging entry to those who could afford to pay and selling tea and cakes to raise money for the local library.

Finn called it 'helping' her in the garden, but in reality he just planted things occasionally. Primroses and roses and hollyhocks, and an unusual variegated tulip. And a peach tree, and the arbutus which did so well in that part of Ireland and which was known affectionately as the strawberry tree.

She had leaned on her spade one day and looked at him. 'Odd choice of plants, Finn.'

'Mmm.'

Something in his tone had set her thinking, set a distant memory jangling in her head, and she'd gone to her computer that evening, when he had gone up to the pub for a pint with Patrick. She'd browsed through her search-engine and had looked up the language of flowers. And there it all was, in black and white before her eyes.

Primrose—fidelity.

Variegated tulip—beautiful eyes.

Peach tree—my heart is thine.

And most lovely of all was the arbutus, which meant esteemed love.

Her eyes had been moist when she'd opened the door to him later.

'You've been crying!' he accused.

'Oh, you stupid man!' she exclaimed, flinging her arms around him. 'Why didn't you tell me?'

'Tell you what?'

'The garden! All those things you planted and I never knew why! Why didn't you just come out and say so?'

'That I love you?' he said tenderly. 'Is that what you want to hear, my sweet, beautiful Catherine?'

'Of course it is!'

They ended up in bed, and afterwards she rolled over to lie on top of him, a fierce look in her eyes. 'Finn?'

'Catherine?'

'Did you ever give another woman flowers with a message?'

'Never.'

'So why me?'

He shrugged, and gave a contented smile which still somehow managed to be edged with sensuality.

'I never wanted to before.'

'Tell me you love me again,' she begged.

'I'll tell you that every day for the rest of our lives,' he promised.

He did. But Catherine had more than words to warm her. She had only to look out at her garden to see Finn's love for her growing every day.

Modern Romance™
...seduction and
passion guaranteed

Tender Romance™
...love affairs that
last a lifetime

Sensual Romance™
...sassy, sexy and
seductive

Blaze™
...sultry days and
steamy nights

Medical Romance™
...medical drama on
the pulse

Historical Romance™
...rich, vivid and
passionate

27 new titles every month.

*With all kinds of Romance for
every kind of mood...*

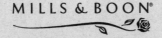

FREE
2 BOOKS
AND A SURPRISE GIFT!

We would like to take this opportunity to thank you for reading this Mills & Boon® book by offering you the chance to take TWO more specially selected titles from the Modern Romance™ series absolutely FREE! We're also making this offer to introduce you to the benefits of the Reader Service™—

- ★ FREE home delivery
- ★ FREE monthly Newsletter
- ★ FREE gifts and competitions
- ★ Exclusive Reader Service discount
- ★ Books available before they're in the shops

Accepting these FREE books and gift places you under no obligation to buy; you may cancel at any time, even after receiving your free shipment. Simply complete your details below and return the entire page to the address below. **You don't even need a stamp!**

YES! Please send me 2 free Modern Romance™ books and a surprise gift. I understand that unless you hear from me, I will receive 4 superb new titles every month for just £2.55 each, postage and packing free. I am under no obligation to purchase any books and may cancel my subscription at any time. The free books and gift will be mine to keep in any case.

P2ZEC

Ms/Mrs/Miss/Mr ....Initials ....
BLOCK CAPITALS PLEASE

Surname ....

Address ....

....

....Postcode ....

Send this whole page to:
UK: FREEPOST CN81, Croydon, CR9 3WZ
EIRE: PO Box 4546, Kilcock, County Kildare (stamp required)